THE *real* HOUSEWIVES OF Adverse City 3

THE *real* HOUSEWIVES OF Adverse City 3

SHELIA E. BELL

www.hispenpublishing.com

Douglasville, Georgia

Cover designed by The Final Wrap
www.thefinalwrap.com

Acknowledgements

I acknowledge you, Father God for being the amazing God that you are. I thank you for your provisions, for your protection, for your power in my life. I thank you because you have blessed me with gifts and talents that are beyond my wildest imagination.

I thank you, God, for loving me enough to bless me with the best sons, grandsons, and great grandchildren in the universe! I thank you for my family and for my friends. I especially thank you for your favor, God, and for your constant provision.

I thank my readers because you continue to support me, believe in me, and push me. Thank you for having the desire to read my work. Thank you for supporting me and encouraging me to keep doing what God has called me to do. I remain eternally grateful.

I thank my editor and publisher, Lacricia A'ngelle, of His Pen Publishing. Lacricia, thank you for your prayers, your belief in what I do and for always giving me a word of inspiration or telling me what 'thus says the Lord.' Thank you for speaking life into me. You are a true gem and one of my dearest and bestest friends in the world. May God richly bless you and pour out blessings in, over, and through your life that you won't have room enough to receive.

"Excellent Reading. I enjoyed all the characters. In this book. It shows that regardless if you are well off financially that if God is not in the midst, you can still be poor in spirit..." Mrs. A.

"I absolutely love this author. Shelia Bell breathes life into every character. By the end of the book, they become friends. And you can't wait to see what they'll be doing next." Kym Hooper-Moore

"I enjoyed both of the books in the series and look forward to the third. They deal with the struggles we have in life, albeit in a more glamorous and sensational way, lol! But I think there were some real nuggets of truth because designer clothes and fancy cars can't cover the ugliness in our hearts. Only God can deal with that." Reviewed by LuvAGoodBook

"I met this author in Memphis a few years ago and was truly impressed with her work. Once I dove into the lives of the housewives. I was freaking hook. She designs every character to leave a permanent stain on your brain. This book was better than watching any reality show on TV. Author Shelia Bell always starts her work off with a fascinating quote to jump start the chapter. These ladies are rich, famous, and scandalous. Each one has secrets and their husbands are no better. From the church to the closet. This book will have you gasping for breath with every page turn. It's a good thing I was behind because I order the sequel as soon as I finish the first one. Love it!" Flenardo

"This book was drama from beginning to end. I don't usually read or watch anything regarding Housewives, but this piqued my interest. Meesha, Peyton, Avery, and Eva had a lot of secrets. Can't wait to read next book." Reviewed by Ms. A

"The Real Housewives of Adversity will give the TV housewives a run for their money in terms of drama without the fist fights. This is part one of the series. I'm awaiting the next installment." Reviewed by Darliss

"Shelia, you have done it again, your writing style, storyline and great details as always is above and beyond . From page one to the end, I was talking to myself and turning the page to see what are they going to do next? I got into each character individually and as couples, the drama and life situations are here and there is a lot!!! Everybody has a separate journey, and I can't wait to see how they handle this."
Reviewed by Sherri Gregory.

IF I TOLD YOU
MY SECRETS,
YOU'D NEVER
LOOK AT ME
THE SAME
AGAIN.

Chapter 1

"God ain't made nobody that he can't handle."
Pastor Gladys Surles

The ladies gathered at Red, The Steakhouse, one of Avery's favorite eateries along St. Pointe Beach. It had been some time since they'd had ladies' day out and the four of them were looking forward to catching up on what had been happening in each of their lives.

Peyton had her driver to bring her to the restaurant since she was still immobile because of her car accident a few months prior.

Meesha arrived first, followed by Peyton, then Avery, and last Eva.

Eva approached the private glass enclosed VIP room of the restaurant where the other three ladies were seated. She walked in wearing large sunglasses and a stylish Stella McCartney jumpsuit.

"Hey, girl," Avery said first, followed by the others.

Eva pulled out her chair and sat down at the table, speaking to each of the housewives.

"Aren't you going to take your glasses off?" Meesha asked.

"I'm good," Eva said. "I have an eye infection and the doctor advised me to keep light away from it as much as possible."

"The lights in here are low. You should be just fine," Peyton said.

"I'd rather not take any chances," replied Eva.

They waited on the servers to bring their appetizers and made small talk during the wait.

"So, how have you been doing, Peyton?" asked Avery.

"I'm good. Just tired of not having the freedom to get around like I want to. But the doctor says it shouldn't be too much longer before I'm able to put weight on my legs."

"That's good," said Meesha.

Peyton, along with the other ladies, sipped mineral water with lemon. She was surprised that she didn't have the hard urge to drink like so many times in the past. Being out in a restaurant, especially one like Red's, was a good test for her. Normally, she would be nursing on at least her third glass of vodka, but the craving was not there today, and for that she felt good.

"Peyton, how is being celibate from drinking coming?" Avery asked, smiling.

"Celibate? From drinking?" Peyton and the other ladies laughed. "Never heard it put quite like that, but to answer your question, I'm good. It's been hard but each day I've managed to fight off the cravings. It may have something to do with the meds they have me on for drinking, and I have to admit that the counselor I talk to everyday has been a lifesaver. Initially, I didn't like the fact that I had to video chat with her every day, but I've come to look forward to it. And she makes an in-home visit once a week, so having someone to talk to who understands alcoholism and the struggles with it, has been a blessing."

"Won't He do it?" Meesha said, and raised a hand in praise at the table. "There's nothing too hard for God. Nothing."

Avery looked at her and slightly rolled her eyes. Meesha didn't seem to notice.

Avery rubbed her protruding belly in a circular motion. "Uhh," she said.

"The baby moved?" Meesha asked, looking at Avery.

"Yeah. This boy is going to be something else," she said.

"I hear you," said Meesha. "But you still don't know what you're having?"

"If you mean have Ryker and I changed our minds about learning the sex of the baby? No we still want it to be a surprise. I just believe that it's a boy. I'm calling those things that are not as though they were," Avery said, trying to quote her own version of a scripture she'd heard in church more than once.

"I started to do that, too but then Carlton and I talked about it and decided we wanted to know the sex of this little booger." Meesha patted her belly and smiled.

"Avery, you're going to be shocked if it's a girl," Eva said. "But I know you won't care, as long as the baby is healthy."

"True," Avery said, nodding. "But I'm telling you, this is a boy."

"If the way you're carrying it is like folks say and like I've experienced, then you probably are having a boy. You're carrying your baby low," Meesha emphasized.

"What does that have to do with anything?" Eva asked, still sitting at the table with her sunglasses on.

"Well, there are several factors that help determine, though it's not actually agreed on by doctors."

"Yeah, it's old wives' tales," Peyton said.

"What? Tell me," Eva said.

"Okay, if you're carrying the baby out front, carrying it low, you didn't suffer from morning sickness in your first trimester, and this one is funny," said Meesha giggling, "if your right breast is bigger than your left, then it's likely you're having a boy."

"I've heard it all," laughed Eva. "We'll see soon enough. So, what does that mean for you, Meesha? Just the opposite I guess."

"Yeah," Peyton teased. "Your big belly is almost up around your neck."

"You could be right but big belly or nah, the ultrasound says it's another hard -headed boy."

"That can still be wrong," added Peyton.

"True that, but we'll see soon enough," Meesha stated, picked of her glass, and took a swallow of water.

The server brought their meals and the ladies continued to laugh and enjoy friendly banter while they dined.

"How much longer before you two drop those loads anyway?" Peyton asked.

"I'm thirty-eight weeks," Meesha said.

"And I'm at thirty-five," Avery said afterwards.

"You have to be forty weeks for delivery, right?" Peyton added.

"Yes, but I have a feeling Ryker the second is coming early."

"Some other old wives' tale gives you reason to think that, too?" asked Eva.

Avery shook her head. "No, I just have a feeling."

"Well, with each of my sons I've carried them to term and for my oldest son, I went past forty weeks!" Meesha said.

"Okay, okay. Enough of the baby talk. Let's get down to some real nitty gritty. What's going on with you and Carlton? How are things on the home front?" Peyton asked curiously while Avery's eyes zeroed in on Meesha.

The ladies waited for Meesha to respond.

"I say things are pretty good. He's doing everything he can to make things right. Ever since I came back from my sister's it's like we're on a second honeymoon or something. Carlton was always attentive even though the church takes a lot of his time. He's always made time for me and the children, but now it's like he's spending even more time with me."

"Does that mean he's satisfying you in the boudoir, too?" Peyton boldly asked.

"Peyton?" Eva said, in an embarrassed sounding tone.

"What? It's not like we're kids here. Is Harper doing you right, Eva?"

"Let's just say that I have no complaints," Meesha spoke up, while Eva almost choked on her mineral water as she took a deep swallow.

"He can be quite ingenious when it comes to that in spite of this big belly." Meesha rubbed her belly, looked down, and smiled before looking back up at the ladies.

"Nobody wants to hear about that," said Avery, almost shouting. The other ladies eyed her rather strangely.

"What's wrong with you?" asked Peyton. "Ryker not handling his business since he got you knocked up?" Peyton and Meesha giggled, while Eva frowned.

"That's none of your business," Avery snapped. "And I don't want to hear about what goes on in any of your bedrooms."

"Since when?" Peyton said.

"Girl, just leave her alone, will you? Can't you see she doesn't want to hear about anything like that." Eva spoke up.

"Like what? Since when did we get all shy about talking about our love lives? You all kill me, acting all brand new!"

"Okay, since you want to talk about love lives, how are you and Derek?" Avery retorted.

Peyton suddenly turned crimson.

"Ohhh, so look who's embarrassed now," Eva said.

"Girl, please," Peyton replied. "I'm not embarrassed about anything."

"Your face looks like a red apple." Avery laughed, joined by the other ladies.

"So what is it? How *are* you and Derek?" Eva asked.

Peyton's expression grew serious and rather sad. "Nothing's changed between us. I mean, he's been really nice and attentive, but we haven't rocked the sheets since way before my accident. I don't know what the future holds for us. I've been praying about it."

"You? Praying?" Avery said smartly.

Peyton rolled her eyes. "He hasn't mentioned divorce anymore and we are rather cordial. I mean, I just pray that what I've done hasn't destroyed my marriage. I love Derek."

"Remember, nothing is impossible with God. I'll continue to pray for you and Derek, and Liam too. How is he, by the way?" Meesha asked, sounding sympathetic.

"He's good. I think our relationship is on the mend. He checks on me before and after school. And sometimes on the weekends, he spends time with me. We may even watch a movie or two. He has asked me on occasion things about his mother, like the kind of person she was before she got strung out on drugs."

"And what do you tell him?" Eva asked.

"I tell him good things, of course. It's not like Breyonna and I were road dawgs or anything like that, but I *did* know her before she got on drugs. She was smart, a little wild, but she had things going for herself. Had she stayed off the drugs, there's no telling what she would have become. But such is life. It happens to some of the best of us."

"Did they ever find anything else about who may have killed her in jail or if it was suicide?" asked Avery.

"Nope, and to be honest, I don't think law enforcement is trying to find anything else out about that. To them she's just another dead dope fiend. It's sad."

"Yeah, that *is* sad," said Eva.

"Well, enough of that talk. Eva, you and Harper still on cloud nine since getting back together?" Meesha asked.

Eva cleared her throat. "Sure, we're good."

"You don't sound too convincing," said Meesha.

"Yeah, are you sure you two are doing okay?" Peyton urged.

"Didn't you hear her? She said they're fine. You all can be so invasive and pushy. Dang," Avery said. "Back off."

"You need to hurry up and drop that load cause you're cranky as all get out!" Peyton retorted.

"I'm just saying, enough is enough."

Silence suddenly filtered around the table while the ladies

focused on their meals. Conversation picked back up toward the end of their meals, but it was mostly about whether or not they would be at church Sunday.

"I plan to be there," Eva said.

"Me too," said Avery.

"Do you think Harper will be there?" Meesha asked. "I know how much you say he hates to miss church."

"He'll miss coming home, but he won't miss attending Perfecting Your Faith unless he has no choice," Eva said, sounding disheartened.

No one responded to her comment. Instead, Peyton said, "I hope me, Derek, and Liam will be there."

"At least you all still come to church as a family as much as possible," said Meesha. "That's a good sign."

"I guess," said Peyton. "I just don't want him doing anything out of pity. You know what I mean?"

"I don't think he's bringing you to church out of pity. Derek doesn't impress me to be like that. If he didn't want to come I think he would come out and say that. He's really a good guy," Meesha said.

"Yeah, he is," said Peyton.

"What about Ryker?" Meesha asked.

"What about Ryker?" repeated Avery.

"I was just asking if you all plan on coming Sunday. You don't have to sound so mean," Meesha said, and frowned slightly.

"As far as I know, we'll be there." Avery looked at her phone. "I have to go. It's almost time to pick up the girls."

The other ladies glanced at their phones.

"Yeah, it's time I head to pick up the boys myself," said Meesha.

They gathered their purses and phones as they ended their ladies' day out.

"It was good to see everybody," Peyton said.

"Is your personal assistant here?" asked Eva.

"Yes, I just texted him. He'll be in here…oh, here he comes," she said, looking up and seeing him walking towards her.

"Where are you headed, Eva?" asked Avery as she stood from the table.

"Oh, you didn't mention when you're starting culinary school," said Peyton.

"That's because you were so busy delving into everybody's bedroom tales," Avery said.

Disregarding her remarks by shooing her off with her hands, she said, "Girl, please. Ryker really needs to give you some. Plus, the last I heard your name is Avery, honey, not Eva."

"Stop it, you two. I start in a few weeks. I can't wait. You ladies were right. It's the best culinary school in Florida, and the South for that matter. I'll keep you all updated on how it goes."

"Okay, and good for you," Meesha said.

"Yeah, we're happy for you," added Avery.

"You're already an excellent cook," Peyton said. "I know you're going to do well."

"Why, thank you, Peyton. That means a lot coming from you."

"Girl, whatever," said Peyton. She looked next to her at her assistant who had appeared. "I'm ready," she said and then headed out of the room, expertly maneuvering her electric wheelchair with the assistant stepping ahead to open the private dining room door for her to exit.

The ladies stopped outside of the restaurant, gave each other hugs and cheek kisses, before departing.

Chapter 2

"Don't tell me of deception; a lie is a lie, whether it be a lie to the eye or a lie to the ear." Samuel Johnson

Screams echoed up and down the hospital corridors sounding like a wounded animal. Meesha had experienced more than her fair share of childbirth. Four times to be exact, but not one of her precious sons had tormented her in labor like this. This little girl was kicking her dead in the—well let's just say it was giving her more than a lady singing the blues.

"Carlton!" she bellowed again and again.

Carlton held on to his wife's hand, allowing her to squeeze it in a death like grip. Sweat poured from Meesha's usually perfectly made up face. Frowns gathered around her eyes and tears gushed forth.

"I'm here, Meesha," Carlton reassured. "Push, baby. Push. He's almost here."

After a seven-hour labor, Meesha screamed and pushed one final time and the precious new life entered the cruel, heartless world.

"It's a girl," the doctor announced as Carlton beamed with the inexplicable joy of having his first daughter. Tears swelled in his own eyes as he looked down at the grayish brown bundle.

The doctor smiled and congratulated the couple. Carlton, with the doctor's assistance, cut the baby's umbilical cord. Afterward, Meesha, with tears streaming down her face, reached out for her daughter and the nurse laid her against Meesha's chest where Meesha cuddled her against her breast and kissed the baby on her forehead. In turn, Carlton kissed Meesha on her forehead and rubbed the sweaty strands of black hair from off her face.

"I love you, Meesha," he mouthed.

"And I love you, Carlton Porter. God got all of this time. No boy like the ultrasound said. Can you believe it? We have a girl, Carlton."

Tears slowly ran down Carlton's cheeks as he leaned down and kissed Meesha on the lips and the tiny newborn on top of her head.

"Isn't our daughter beautiful?"

"Yes, sweetheart, she is. Our first daughter. She's perfect."

Meesha studied the little human and smiled between her own tears. "Yes, she is perfect in every way. "

"We're going to name her Makena Grace, right? You said if we ever had a daughter that would be her name."

"Yes. It's the perfect name for a perfect baby," Meesha said, staring at her bundle of joy.

"She's just as beautiful as her mother." Carlton continued staring at his wife and newborn daughter in total adoration.

Nurses then whisked her off to the other side of the room where they poked, preened, cleaned, and weighed her while she wailed.

"Nine pounds, ten ounces," one of the nurses said to the other. After they were done, one of the nurses brought the precious little one back over to her waiting parents.

Carlton reached for his daughter wrapped in a pink nursey blanket and matching cap. He stared at her until Meesha interrupted.

"Bring her closer, Carlton." He held her until the nurse

informed him that they would be taking Meesha to her room and the baby for examination.

Once inside her room, Carlton sat down and Meesha quickly fell asleep in exhaustion. Without warning, his mind fell on Avery and her unborn child. The two of them had not spoken to each other personally, other than an occasional handshake at church. But for the past few weeks, Avery hadn't been attending church. He learned from overhearing Meesha talking to one of the housewives that Avery had been placed on bedrest until the birth of her child.

Carlton continued to be concerned about whether the baby she was carrying was his or not. It was definitely a possibility, but he had been praying and asking God to not let it be his kid. He already felt extremely blessed when it was revealed through DNA testing that Peyton's son, Liam, was not his biological kid. He reasoned with God again, praying if God allowed his affair with Avery to remain under wraps, he would be devoted to Meesha and the boys, and now their daughter as well.

As if reading his thoughts, Carlton's phone text chimed. I think I might be going into labor. Waiting on Ryker to get home. Thought real baby daddy would want to know.

Carlton cussed underneath his breath. Why was she contacting him? He looked over at Meesha sleeping before stepping out of her hospital room to call Avery. No answer. He called again. No answer. He followed up with a text. I will be praying for you and your baby. God bless you, Sister Avery.

Chapter 3

"The first step towards getting somewhere is to decide you're not going to stay where you are." John Morgan

Eva toured the culinary school with a sense of heightened anticipation for the independence becoming a chef could possibly give her. She was tired of being dependent on Harper. He continued to make sure she never forgot that if it wasn't for him her family in Bolivia would still be severely destitute.

She had made her share of mistakes and she was sorry that she cheated on him, but it wasn't like Harper gave her the time, attention, and affection she yearned for. She loved her husband, and she wanted to spend as much time with him as she possibly could. Returning to their home sometimes felt like a mistake but what real choice did she have? If she divorced him she would get nothing. She would be left alone, without a penny to her name. She couldn't go back to the life she used to live. She felt so stupid. She should have denied everything especially after learning that she wasn't pregnant. But, *noooo*, when Harper accused her of cheating, she cowered down.

She was glad that she had taken the girls' advice and sought out the best culinary school in Miami. When she told Harper about it, he was all for it. He said he would pay for it and hoped she would take advantage of his generosity. He was always telling her that she needed to find a hobby or something to past the time because his life was full and he didn't have a lot of time to spend with her.

His life being 'full' was an understatement, because in addition to being Chief Medical Director at Adverse General Hospital, he had returned to filming his television show, *The Heart of the Matter*. The show had been successful in the past and showcased his skill as a respected, renowned heart surgeon. He invited guests on the show that had gone through traumatic events, heart surgery, or life altering situations that were often quite touching and inspirational.

Some of the past television shows brought Eva to tears with the real life people and sometimes heartbreaking situations that people faced. Added to that was Harper's flourishing writing career. He had written two more books and was working on a third for his publisher. The books, like the television show, centered on various things about how to keep the heart healthy through proper diet, exercise, and mindset. Harper was a genius in his own right. Who was she to interfere with a man of his status and caliber? She felt both lucky and blessed that he even wanted her.

After committing adultery, she thought their marriage was over, but Harper had given her another chance, and she didn't want to blow it. Being somewhat religious, he told her that it was God who told him to forgive her and give his marriage another go. Thank God Harper wasn't aware that it was Seth that she'd slept with—no way would he have wanted her back.

"How do you think you're going to like culinary school?" Peyton asked when Eva called her after returning from her school tour.

"I think it'll be fun. I'm really excited. Like you and the others said, I can open my own restaurant. Who knows, I may become a Michelin Chef or even an Iron Chef one day." Eva giggled into the phone.

"You're right. Think big, girl. Are you going to come by here?" Peyton asked.

"You know Meesha had the baby this morning."

"Yes, I read the group text she sent," Peyton answered. "She has a baby girl. That's so cool. I'm happy for her and Carlton."

"Me too. I know she's on cloud nine. Well, I planned on going to the hospital to see her and the baby."

"Oh, okay. I'm so bored. I can't wait until I can get out of this chair, walk again, and do things on my own. I hate having to depend on Derek or one of these nurses for everything. And my poor son, I know he has to get tired of waiting on me hand and foot."

"That boy loves you, Peyton. You're his mother, and it's not like he's waiting on you hand and foot. You have the best of care, your own personal chef, a nurse at your beck and call, and Derek gives you as much attention as he can. You're lucky, girl. I wish Harper spent half as much time with me as Derek does with you."

"That's only because he's doing what he thinks he needs to do as my husband. You and I both know that as soon as I can fully take care of myself, he's out of here again. He's going to divorce me and I can't say I blame him."

"Look, listen to what Meesha, Avery…*and I* keep telling you. You still have a chance to save your marriage. Derek didn't come back home because he feels sorry for you—the man still loves you. He just wants you to stop drinking, and thank God you have. How long has it been now since you last had a drink?"

"Too long," Peyton quickly answered. "Seriously, it's been about six months. I can't have one even if I wanted to. With these pop up tests and visits by my alcohol and drug counselor, I can hardly piss without someone knowing. And the meds they have me taking can make me deathly ill if I so much as sip on a cooler."

"You know it's for your own good, Peyton." Eva walked to

her car, climbed inside, and sat in the parking lot of the elite culinary school, talking to Peyton until another call came through. It was from an unfamiliar number but it had the Adverse General Hospital prefix. "Hold on a minute. This might be Harper calling."

Eva switched the call over. "Hello."

I had the baby," Avery said, whispering into the phone.

"Avery?"

"Yeah, it's me. I just had the baby," Avery repeated.

"You what?" squealed Eva. "When, how, I mean what, oooh, oh, I mean you weren't due for several weeks."

"I know, tell that to my son," Avery said.

"A boy? You had a boy?"

"Yep, I told you all it was going to be a boy."

"I know you did, but you said you didn't want to know until you had the baby."

"Uh, exactly...and I have a boy." Avery laughed.

"How is he? How are you?"

"I'm good, but he's in NICU."

"NICU? Why? What's going on?" Eva asked, trying to maintain her composure so she wouldn't upset Avery.

"He has a pretty bad case of jaundice and since he was born a little early they're keeping an eye on him for a few hours. He should be able to come into my room a little later this afternoon. I just wanted to let you know I had him."

"Where is Ryker?"

"He went to NICU to see if there have been any changes."

"And Lexie and Heather. How are they?

"Oh, the girls, they're good. They're still at school," Avery said, sounding somewhat sad.

"Are you okay? You don't sound like someone who just gave birth to her first son. I know you and Ryker have to be thrilled," Eva said as she started the car and headed out of the parking lot and onto the street.

"I'm okay. Just worried about my baby."

"You shouldn't be. You said he's going to be fine."

"Yeah, I know, but I'm still concerned. He weighed five pounds, two ounces, and he's seventeen and a half inches. He's such a little thing. Anyway, will you tell everyone for me?"

"Sure, I will. I don't know if you saw her text, but Meesha delivered earlier this morning, and now you've had yours. How weird is that?" Eva said, laughing into the phone.

"No, I didn't get a text. Are you sure?"

"Yes, I'm sure. She sent out a group text. You were probably in labor when she sent it," Eva chuckled. "What did she have?" Avery asked.

"She had a little girl. I was going to go see her and the baby later this afternoon. I just came back from touring the culinary institute. I start school next week."

"Good for you. You're going to do well. I just know it. So you were coming to see Meesha later, huh?"

"Yeah, I don't know why I assumed you knew that she had the baby. I'll stop by to see you, too. You two are probably on the same floor in the Maternity Unit, right?"

"Yes, uh, of course. I'm in suite 2996."

"Meesha's in…I think Carlton told me it was Suite 3201. Anyway, I'll see you a little later. I'm going to run by the house, change clothes, and then I'll be on my way. I know you have to be tired. Giving birth takes a lot out of you, I'm sure."

"Yeah, it does, but I've been around the block a couple of times, so I'm good. Just worried about my son."

"Don't worry. Try to get some rest. I'll see you later. Oh, yeah and Avery?"

"Yes, Eva?"

"Congratulations! I'm happy for you and Ryker. You didn't tell me the baby's name."

"What else would it be? Ryker the second." Avery faintly smiled into the phone, while silently wishing she could have named the baby after Carlton.

"Ryker has himself a junior," Eva said. "Good for him. I'll see you later," Eva said. "Oh gosh, I forgot, I have Peyton on the other end. I'll talk to you later."

"Okay, bye, Eva."

Eva clicked over but Peyton had already hung up. Peyton would never hold on when people called her and put her on hold. She felt that it was so inappropriate, yet Peyton had no problem putting someone else on hold.

"I'll call her back in a few minutes," Eva said aloud as she drove toward her residence. She smiled at the thought of both Meesha and Avery having their babies on the same day and hours apart. That was so far-fetched to her. Her feeling of happiness was replaced with overwhelming sadness as she thought about her false pregnancy. She so wanted to have a child to love and care for, but as long as she was married to Harper she knew that would never be a possibility.

Harper's secret about his vasectomy had taken her for a loop, literally knocked the wind out of her. Then when the doctor told her that she wasn't pregnant, it was another huge blow. She could still see herself in the doctor's office that day, hearing his devastating words. *"There's no easy way to say this, but there is no fetus, Mrs. Stenberg. The pregnancy tests you took were false positives. You have what's called polycystic ovary syndrome."*

Unless she left Harper or somehow persuaded him to adopt a kid, she would forever be childless as long as she was married to him. Tears poured from her shapely dark eyes. She wiped her tears away with one hand while keeping her other hand braced on the steering wheel. If only she could talk Harper into getting his vasectomy reversed so they could try to have a child. But Eva knew that would probably be close to impossible because Harper made it clear that he was not ready to have a kid. His life was centered around his career. He didn't have the time to give her, so he definitely didn't want a kid running around under foot.

Eva arrived at the hospital, stopped in the hospital gift shop, and picked out gifts for Meesha and Avery. She asked to have Avery's gifts and flowers delivered to her room and she carried Meesha's with her since she was going to visit her first.

When she entered the room, Meesha was breastfeeding her new little bundle of joy.

"Hi, Eva, come in," Meesha greeted her when the door opened and she saw that it was Eva. "I'm so glad you came."

"Hey, girl. I told you I would be here." She walked up to her and looked down at the suckling baby girl with a head full of thick, curly black hair. She placed the flowers and stuffed baby bear on the table next to Meesha's bed.

"The flowers are beautiful and look at the cute little stuffed bear. Thank you."

"You're welcome. So, how are you?"

"I'm good."

Eva studied the little bundle with intensity. "Meesha, she is so beautiful." Eva was overcome with happiness at seeing the newborn. She fought back tears as she tried to push the thought of her not having children out of her mind.

"Ohhh, it's okay, Eva. Don't cry. Please don't cry."

"I can't help it. I'm so happy for you and Carlton. By the way, where is Carlton?"

"He just left a little while ago. He'll be back later."

"How long will you be in the hospital?"

"I'll probably be going home tomorrow, I'm sure. You know they don't keep you in the hospital for long these days, especially after having a baby. If there are no complications, they'll boot you out of here in a heartbeat. Plus, you know I *am* somewhat of a pro at this," Meesha said and laughed.

"Wow, I didn't know you would go home that quickly. Did you know that Avery is down the hall?"

"No, I didn't. What happened? Is she all right?"

"Yes, she had the baby."

"What? Is the baby okay?"

"Yes, she says the baby is fine, just a case of jaundice. I'm going to go see her when I leave you."

Meesha laughed slightly. "Can you believe it? Me and Avery's kids born minutes or hours apart. That's cool."

"Yeah, I think so, too. Makes it easier for birthday parties, huh?"

"You got that right. What did she have?" asked Meesha.

"A boy, just like she predicted. I'm happy for her."

"I know she's happy about that. She and Ryker wanted a son so badly. God is so good. And if the baby has jaundice, that shouldn't be hard to clear up. He'll be fine."

"Yeah, I'm sure you're right, but Avery sounded upset when I talked to her. I could hear it in her voice."

"Well, you and I both know that it doesn't take much to upset Avery. She's sensitive like that and she's definitely a worrier. She stresses about the least of things. I'll say a prayer for her and the baby."

"That's sweet of you, Meesha."

"That's what friends do."

"Yeah, you're right. I just can't get over how beautiful she is, and she's so tiny."

"She's going to be spoiled rotten. I already know," Meesha said. "The boys wanted a sister. Carlton and I wanted a little girl, so you know we are going to treat little Miss Makena Grace like a true princess."

"Makena Grace? Is that her name?" Eva asked.

"Yes. You like it?"

"Yes, I love it. It sounds so graceful and elegant. Like a real princess' name."

Meesha smiled. "Thanks. It's a name I always said I would name my daughter if I ever had one, and now look at her, Eva. I have my very own little princess."

Meesha's baby began to release the cutest little cry as she stopped nursing.

"Is she all right?" asked Eva, looking at the little girl with curiosity and concern.

"Yes, she's fine. She's already vocal, telling me what she wants." Meesha smiled and then whispered sweet words to the little girl, kissed her on top of her head, and then sat up farther in the bed so she could burp her.

Eva watched every move. *Oh, God, why not me? Why not me?*

Chapter 4

"A friend is not only someone who you can confide in, it is someone who can mirror the trust you have shown by confiding in you as well." Ashley Young

Avery lay in the hospital room in tears. A gamut of emotions rushed through her mind. Her baby boy was born several weeks early, but the doctor reassured her that other than jaundice, the child appeared to be healthy. He was still in NICU for observation and Avery couldn't wait to hold the baby she prayed was Carlton's son, in her arms.

After visiting Meesha and her baby, Eva walked down the hall to see Avery and her baby. When she stepped inside the room, it was dark and eerily quiet. Unlike when she visited Meesha, she didn't see Avery's baby in the room. Eva walked over to Avery's bed. Her head was turned toward the window and she appeared to be soundly sleeping.

Eva turned to leave but Avery called out in a low voice. "Eva, is that you?"

Eva stopped, turned, and looked around, "Yes, it's me. I didn't mean to wake you. Get your rest. I'll come back later."

"No, don't leave. I want you to stay."

Eva walked back over to her best friend out of all the

housewives. She kissed her on the cheek and then reached down to squeeze her hand. "Are you feeling okay?"

"Yeah, I'm okay. I just wish my son was in here with me."

"How long will it be before they bring him in? Has he even been in here yet?"

"No, he hasn't. I hope they'll bring him in later this evening. They said he's doing well. He's under that special light they use for babies with jaundice. Can you believe it, Eva? I have a son." A smile filled Avery's face and tears crested in the corner of her eyes.

"I'm happy for you, and I can't imagine how proud Ryker must be."

"Yes, he sure is. He went to check on Heather and Lexie. He'll be back later on. That leaves us time to talk. I need someone I can talk to that I can trust." Avery's facial expression turned deftly serious. "And you're my best friend. You're the only one I feel I can confide in, and you don't judge me. I love you for that, Eva." Avery wiped tears from her eyes with the back of her hand before they fell.

"You're my best friend, too. I don't know what I would do if I didn't have you. I left everything when I came to the States. My friends, my family, all so I could be with Harper and give my family a better life. I don't have anyone in the States that I'm closer to than you. Meeting you has been such a blessing. Always know that I'm here for you, Avery. Tell me, what is it? You know you can talk to me about anything."

"I don't know where to start," Avery mumbled.

"Start from the beginning, the end, the middle, wherever you want to start. Just start. You look troubled and I have a feeling that something isn't right. Are you and Ryker having problems again?"

"No, it's nothing like that. We couldn't be better, but depending on the decision I make all that could change in a New York minute."

"Huh, a New York minute? I don't follow," Eva said, as her eyebrows furrowed.

"That means things could change in a second. Anyway, for now it's not Ryker. Our marriage is stable. It's someone else."

"What do you mean, it's someone else? Is it the kids? Your family? What is it? Tell me, Avery. You're scaring me."

"It's…it's Carlton."

"Huh, Carlton? Carlton, who?"

How many Carltons do you know, Eva? Pastor Carlton Porter."

"What about him? Has he done something to Meesha?"

"Not directly, but then again, maybe. You see," Avery spoke slowly and cautiously, "my baby might be Carlton's son."

"What did you just say?"

"You heard me. There's a possibility that Ryker is not my baby's father. It might be Carlton's child."

Eva reeled and had to steady herself by grabbing hold of the food table at the end of Avery's bed. She used one hand to grab her head like she was trying to keep from fainting.

"Are you okay?" Avery asked. "Go over there and sit down." She pointed to the chair near the window and on the other side of the bed.

Eva walked slowly around and over to the chair and sat in it. "How? I mean, when? I'm so confused. I don't understand."

"Please, you can't say a word to anyone. If this gets out, it could ruin everything for me and any future I might have with Carlton…or Ryker."

"You know I wouldn't say anything. Just tell me what this is all about." Eva wiped her forehead as if she was sweating; when actually she was developing a headache that she knew had to be nothing more than from stress. So much had been going on in her own life. There was so much that she was facing that she hadn't told Avery, her family, or anyone about. Yet, here Avery was confiding in her that she had slept with Carlton Porter? This pushed her stress level to the max, but she had to keep it together for her best friend's sake.

"Do you want to hear what happened?"

Eva nodded. "Yes. Of…course." She spoke slow and deliberate as her head began to pound like it had a heartbeat of its own.

"Okay. Here goes. Carlton and I began an affair shortly after my suicide attempt. You remember when I went into counseling with him?"

Eva nodded, unable to speak. It was if her tongue was tied.

"You know back then Ryker and I were having our share of problems. I was still hurt about him cheating on me with my cousin. I felt inadequate, lower than low. Added to that, he didn't act like he loved me. I thought he couldn't put behind my past life as a call girl. It was just everything mounting up and I couldn't take it anymore. I wanted out. I thought the girls, my family, and Ryker, would be better off without me, but I even botched that up. I felt absolutely horrible. Being my pastor, Carlton came to the hospital to visit. He prayed with me, talked to me, and coupled with seeing a therapist, I began to feel somewhat better, but I was still a mess. He suggested that I make an appointment for one-on-one counseling if I felt like I needed to talk to someone after I was discharged from the hospital. When I mentioned it to Ryker, he agreed that it might be a good thing to talk to Carlton from a spiritual standpoint. I reluctantly agreed. When I went to talk to him, I found Carlton was really easy to talk to, and he's a great listener, too. I began to look forward to our sessions. One day, I broke down. I couldn't stop crying after expressing my thoughts and feelings to him about my life and all of the mistakes I'd made."

"Don't tell me. I know the scenario. One thing led to another." Eva shook her head from side to side and slightly rolled her eyes.

"I guess I was wrong when I said you wouldn't judge me. Looks like you are doing just that," Avery said.

"I'm not judging you, Avery. I'm thinking about Carlton Porter. He is a man who you should have been able to trust."

"I *could* trust him and I *did* trust him. He consoled me that day, and I don't care what you think about it, one thing really did lead to another. He told me how beautiful I was, how much I had going for me. He told me the mistakes of the past couldn't erase the fact that I was a wonderful person who deserved love. He convinced me God had forgiven me for all of my sins and all of the terrible mistakes I'd made. When he kissed me on the cheek and hugged me, neither of us expected or meant for anything more to happen—but it did. That kiss on the cheek led to us kissing one another. There was an attraction that neither of us could deny. It felt right. For the first time in a long time, I felt desired, Eva. I felt that someone truly wanted me. Ryker and I only slept together when he was horny and even then, he didn't put his all into it. I felt so used by him, but with Carlton, things felt, well, it felt different. That's the only way I can explain it."

"What about Meesha, Avery? Meesha is your friend, and you of all people know how it feels to be cheated on. Look at how it almost destroyed you and your marriage. Look at what happened with Harper and me."

"I know all that, and I hear what you're saying, but Meesha didn't deserve to be with Carlton. I still feel that way. I know I should have thought about her, but I didn't; I couldn't. All I could think about was being held in Carlton's arms. All I thought about was the next time I would see him."

"You made love in his office? Please tell me that he at least respected you enough to take you to a hotel."

"The first time we were in his office. After that, we met at a hotel. It doesn't matter where we met. What matters is I fell in love with him and he fell in love with me. Then all of that mess about Liam came up and that caused a huge distraction in our relationship. He was going to divorce Meesha and I was going to leave Ryker. We were going to be together, but everything unraveled. It all fell apart because of the Liam situation. Carlton told me that we had to call things off, and then Meesha went and got herself pregnant." Anger began to surface in Avery's voice. Her eyes tightened, her brows wrinkled, and her lips turned downward as she spoke with force.

"I almost hated her when I found out she was pregnant."

"That's why you've been treating her so cold?"

Avery nodded. "I guess. It's just that she always pretends like she's Miss Perfect when really all she's good for is making babies. Carlton felt he was trapped, too. He told me so. He said he stopped loving Meesha a long time ago, but because of the kids and because of his position in the church, he felt he had to stay in the marriage…until he and I got together."

"I can't believe what I'm hearing," Eva said, looking intensely at Avery. "Sounds like he was more than a good listener and counselor. He sounds like a cheating, smooth talking, trickster."

"Don't make fun of the situation, Eva. Please. You of all people should know what loneliness can do. Ryker wasn't exactly a model husband at the time. Learning that he slept with my cousin almost destroyed my life. I know I was partially the blame for offering him a ménage a trois, but still, I didn't expect him to happily run off and screw my own cousin. Anyway, Carlton and I fell in love and then I got pregnant. I…I…"

"Fell in love? Are you serious? Does he even know that this could be his child?"

Avery nodded. "Yes, of course, he does."

"What did he say? I mean are you going to tell Ryker? Is Carlton going to tell Meesha? Are you going to have a DNA test?"

"He says he doesn't think the baby is his and maybe he's right. He barely says a thing to me now. He won't answer my texts or return my calls—and it's all because of Meesha. Why did she have to go and get pregnant? She should have stayed away and never came back to Adverse City."

"Stayed away? What are you talking about?" Eva frowned.

"You know when she left him and went to visit her sister. She was planning to leave him and not come back. I know it, but then she had to waltz her skinny behind back to town and it ruined every chance of us being together."

"You just said it was Liam and the possibility that he was Carlton's kid that messed things up between you two." Eva was beginning to feel sorry for Avery. Avery wasn't thinking right. She needed real counseling, someone who could help her get her emotions and her mind stable again. Avery was such a kind and wonderful person. Eva hated to see her confused like she was. And Carlton? How could he do this? He was supposed to be a leader, a confidante, but he was nothing more than a *lobo vestido con ropa de oveja, a wolf dressed in sheep's clothing*, she thought.

"Why does she always have to win?"

"Avery, listen to me. This is not Meesha's fault." Eva rose from the chair and walked over and stood next to the bed. "Listen to yourself. You're talking about another woman's husband. He can't be yours. He doesn't belong to you. It's not right. You know that. You wouldn't want to hurt Meesha like that. It's not the kind of person you are. Meesha has done nothing to you. She doesn't deserve a scumbag like Carlton and neither do you."

"You're only saying this because you don't understand what Carlton and I shared, Eva. It's Meesha's fault. All of this is Meesha's fault. As for a DNA test, I don't know what I'm going to do. Ryker and I are in such a good place. There's more that I haven't told you."

"How much more could there be?" Eva was stunned at hearing Avery tell her about having an affair with Carlton. All this time she had looked up to the man and highly respected him. Did Meesha know he had been cheating on her? Is that why she left Carlton? Avery says it was the reason Carlton asked Meesha for a divorce over a year ago. Then he changed his mind and wanted his marriage to work. Everything was so crazy. None of it made sense. Avery kept talking, this time Eva felt like she would pass out.

"Ryker and I were never married. I was living a lie all of this time, that is until lately."

Eva took a step backwards, away from the side of Avery's bed, and sat back down. "What?"

"What I'm telling you is that Ryker and I were only legally married a few months ago. It was grand. He flew me to Las Vegas and we had the most beautiful private ceremony a girl could ask for." Avery smiled like she had forgotten all about what she'd just told Eva about her and Carlton.

"You and Ryker were never married?"

"Nope. But we are now, and that's why I'm so confused. I don't know what to do. I want my marriage to work for the sake of the children but part of me is still in love with Carlton."

Eva rose from the chair again and stood next to Avery's bed.

"Listen, Avery. Think about this. You can't give up your marriage and your children for Carlton. And you know the last thing he'll do is leave Meesha. He's proven that to you. They just got back together."

"They only got back together because she told him she was pregnant! Don't you understand that? Haven't you heard anything I've said? That hussy knew exactly what she was doing. She knew the only thing that would make him stay with her would be to have another kid. Carlton loves *me*. He wants *us* to be together." Avery began to get upset all over again. She had just given birth to a child that she sincerely believed belonged to Carlton and yet here she was trying to defend him for staying with Meesha. It wasn't fair. None of this was fair.

"Avery, listen to yourself. For God's sake, you and Meesha just gave birth a few hours ago. You can't expect or even think that a man like Carlton Porter would leave his ministry, his family, his wife, for…for—"

"For what, Eva? For some mixed up chick like me?"

"No, that's not what I was going to say. I mean the same thing goes for you. You can't jeopardize what you have with Ryker because of some fling you had with Carlton. Think about it. Ryker could take the kids from you. He's a powerful, well-respected attorney. You would lose everything. And if you two have just gotten married then why would you want that to end? None of this makes sense, Avery."

"It may not make sense, but it's all true." Avery began crying. "I don't know what to do. I've messed up my life over and over again. Now I've brought another innocent child in this world but this time, it may not even be my husband's baby. And Carlton, I thought he loved me. He said he was going to divorce Meesha and we would be together, but then when I told him I was pregnant, he dumped me faster than a hot potato. Oh, Eva, please tell me what to do."

Eva leaned in and hugged her friend. How could she tell her what to do when her own life was in shambles? "Look, why don't you try to get some rest before they bring the baby in here. You're going to need it. Don't worry or think about that louse, Carlton Porter. He doesn't deserve your time. He doesn't deserve a wonderful person like you, Avery." Eva began to tear up. "You're my best friend. I hate to see you hurting like this. You deserve so much better. You're an amazing woman, a great mother, and the best friend a girl could have. Don't waste your love on someone like Carlton. Think about Meesha, Avery. Think how this would destroy her if she ever found out about you and Carlton. It would tear her apart, and she doesn't deserve that. Neither of you deserve to be hurt by that man."

Avery listened and tears streamed down her face. "Maybe you're right. Meesha doesn't deserve to be hurt and neither do I. I don't know what I was thinking. How can he love me? I'm probably not the first woman he's stepped out on his marriage with. What about that woman, Liam's biological mother? He was probably smashing her too. I've been so blind, Eva."

"Maybe you have, Avery, but thank God, now you see."

Chapter 5

"All relationships go through hell, real ones get through it."
Heartfelt quotes

Peyton sat outside, in the large open area, in front of the infinity pool, while she patiently waited for her water therapy session to start. Getting in the salt-water pool made her feel relaxed. The water was warm and refreshing. She was thankful that she could live the kind of life she was living and have money of her own. Whether Derek walked out of her life or not, she was more than financially self-sufficient. The thing is she wanted her marriage to work. It was not about who had the most money. Sure, Derek had become quite successful and beyond rich. His money could easily rival the money from her long stream of family money, but what she wanted was her husband, her son, and a happy life with the man who she had given her heart to fourteen years ago.

"How are you this afternoon?" Derek walked up behind her, startling her.

Peyton whipped around in the electric chair. She'd become somewhat of a pro at maneuvering it.

"Hi. I'm good. Sitting out here waiting on Sharon and Jack to get here for my water therapy. What's up?"

"Just thought I'd come by and check on you between

meetings." Derek looked at her and it almost made Peyton feel somewhat uneasy.

"What is it? You're looking at me like you have something on your mind. Say what it is."

"Everything's good. I do want to tell you that I'm proud of you. You're working really hard. I've spoken to the therapists. They say you're progressing faster than expected. Hopefully, you'll be able to get up out of that chair and start putting some weight on your legs in a couple weeks."

"Yeah, that's what the orthopedic doctor says. I'm doing everything he tells me to do, and this water therapy really does help."

"As for your drinking or should I say not drinking, I'm impressed with that, too. Your alcohol counselor says you're following the program to a tee. That's good to hear. You look better, your mood is brighter, and your complexion is almost glowing."

Peyton smiled. "Thanks. I'm glad you feel like that. I am working hard. I know I've been a big disappointment to you and to our son, and I can't stop telling you how sorry I am. I've messed up royally, Derek, and I know that. For God's sake, I could have lost my life or be a cripple for the rest of my life, but God saw fit, for whatever reason, to save me. Now I have another chance. For that, I'm grateful. I know you aren't in love with me anymore, and I'm coming to terms with that too. Do I want our marriage to work? Yes. Would I like us to be one big happy family like we used to be so many years ago? Of course. But I'm no fool either. My counselor has helped me realize a lot of things about myself. One thing I've learned is that before I can truly love someone else, or be good to or for someone else, I have to learn how to love *me*." Peyton pointed to herself and then continued talking. "Drinking gave me a means of escape. An escape from all of the things I'd done, like when I took Liam. I've done so much wrong, Derek, and having a ton of money doesn't, or can't, erase it because it's forever etched in my mind. I think about the way I've treated, or should I say mistreated you, over the years. You're a good man and I have never deserved you, but I can't turn back the hands of time. I can do nothing to change the past. All I can do is try to make sure Liam has a better future."

"You don't have to say all of this now, Peyton. Just continue to work on you. Believe it or not, I'm not perfect either." He chuckled.

"Really?" Peyton said and laughed herself. "I thought you were the one who does everything oh so right."

"I wish," Derek replied. "I haven't always been the best husband. I've fallen short in supporting you. I guess I found it easier to point the finger at you for all the wrong things you did instead of looking at myself and trying to be a better man, a better husband, and a better friend. Anyway, it is what it is, and for what it's worth, I don't hate you, Peyton. I care about you. I care about you a lot."

"I believe that, Derek."

Derek looked at his Apple watch. "I better head back to the bank and get prepared for this meeting. Liam should be home soon."

"Yeah, he's at lacrosse practice. He's really excelling in the sport." Peyton smiled proudly.

"Yes, he is. That's our kid. I'm proud of him."

"Me, too."

"Excuse me, Mrs. Hudson; are you ready to start your session?" Sharon walked out to the pool area and asked.

"Hi, Sharon," said Derek.

"Hello, Mr. Hudson."

Hi, Sharon. Hello, Jack. Jack appeared behind Sharon.

"Hello, Mr. and Mrs. Hudson," Jack said.

"Your wife is doing great with her therapy, Mr. Hudson," Sharon commented.

"She swims like a fish," added Jack.

"I'm glad to hear that. Do you think she'll be able to start putting weight on her legs anytime soon?"

"I'm only the therapist," said Sharon, "but I've seen enough of these types of injuries to be able to say I think in the next couple of weeks, she should be able to start putting weight on them. The water is good and you all are fortunate to have this warm salt-water pool. It's good for Mrs. Hudson. It has helped speed up her recovery. Everyone isn't so blessed," said Sharon.

Peyton nodded.

"Well, I've got to get out of here. Have a good session." Derek walked over to Peyton and kissed her lightly on the cheek, surprising her.

It had been months since he had touched her and Peyton longed for his expert lovemaking. She wanted to feel needed, loved, and desired again. It was during moments like this when she would turn to drinking to shield the desires burning inside, but that was in the past. She was determined not to put another alcoholic beverage of any kind up to her lips ever again. Only God would be able to hold her to that promise.

"See you tonight, that is, if you plan on coming home for dinner," she suggested.

Since he and Liam moved back in the house, Derek spent little time having family dinners. There were days he would meet Liam at some restaurant for dinner or he would bring home something but as for the three of them spending family time together, it was basically nonexistent. Peyton told herself that she should be satisfied that he and Liam had moved back into the house, even if it was only because of her accident that he'd returned. She missed their past life together, imperfect as it was, but she was determined not to force Derek into anything. Her counselor reiterated that she had to work on herself and everything else would have its proper place. Peyton prayed that the counselor knew what she was talking about.

"I'm not sure," was Derek's response. "I'll call or text you and let you know. If I do come home, I'll be sure to let the chef know to prepare enough for me. Anything particular you want?"

"Not really. You know me, I can always eat pasta."

Derek smiled that handsome, captivating smile that Peyton had come to love and adore. She smiled back. "Okay, just let me know."

"I will. Have a good session," he said. "Thanks again for helping my wife," he said to Sharon and Jack before disappearing inside the house with Peyton's eyes glued on his perfect physique. "Let's get this party started," she turned and said to the therapists when he was beyond her view.

"Let's do it," said Sharon. Jack and Sharon walked up to Peyton when she got next to the pool. Jack made sure the motorized lifter was in the right position. Once she was on it, she removed her mobilizers, and then secured herself with the strap on the lifter. Jack placed the attached remote control inside Peyton's hand.

Peyton maneuvered the lifter until she was over the pool and then pressed the Down lever to lower herself into the warm water. Sharon got in the pool while Jack remained out of the pool until Peyton was in the water deep enough. Sharon stood next to Peyton for support while Peyton moved off of the chair lifter and was in the five feet deep water.

They began her therapy and for the next hour they worked harder than ever.

When she was done, Peyton reached for the remote, lowered the chair down low enough for her to get back in the seat and bring her out of the water. She transitioned back into her chair.

"Great job," said Jack.

"You are one determined lady," Sharon praised.

"I have to be. I have a full life I want to live," Peyton said. "I've been given another chance. I don't want to blow it."

"Good for you," Sharon said while Jack walked over to

the towel rack and returned with a large towel and handed it to Peyton. Peyton dried herself off. When she was done, she headed toward the pool house where she had things set up inside to take a shower.

"We're going to rest and in about thirty minutes, we'll go inside the main house and start on your other leg exercises," Sharon told her.

"If you don't mind, I'd like to do them out here this afternoon. It's such a beautiful day and the view of the ocean is breathtaking. I love being out here. It revitalizes me and gives me renewed energy."

"I have no problem with that," Sharon said. "Do you, Jack?"

"I'm all for it. Mrs. Hudson's right; it's like a slice of heaven out here."

"Mrs. Hudson, would you like a snack before you start your next session?" her personal chef appeared and asked.

"I think I would. Could you prepare some light sandwiches, enough for me, Sharon, and Jack?"

"Of course. I've already made a fresh pitcher of lemonade if you'd like me to bring it out."

"You read my mind. Yes, please bring it on out."

The chef turned and walked back inside. Moments later, while Sharon and Jack did some light exercises with Peyton, the chef returned with a tray of delicious looking finger sandwiches and the pitcher of fresh squeezed lemonade.

Liam entered the massive family room where he found his mother sitting in front of the television. "Dad just texted me. He says to tell you that he has to work late and won't be home for dinner."

Disappointed, Peyton said, "Awe, I hate to hear that. I was hoping the three of us could enjoy a meal together. But I'm sure if he could be here he would."

"Yeah," said, Liam. "I'm going to eat in my room. If that's

okay with you."

"Honey, I was hoping that you would at least stay and eat with me."

"If you really want me to I will, but I wanted to chill and watch this movie on Netflix. You don't like thrillers so I know you wouldn't be interested."

Peyton smiled slightly. "Go ahead, enjoy yourself. Will you go in the kitchen and tell Mrs. Garcia to whip up something quick and easy. Let her know your father won't be joining us, too."

"Sure, Mom."

Liam disappeared, leaving Peyton alone with her thoughts and her desire for a drink that was growing stronger by the minute. It was times like this that the desire for alcohol hit her hardest. Being left alone, feeling rejected by the very ones she loved, was hard to take. Derek told her he would call or text her, but instead he called Liam, anything to keep from talking directly to her. At least that's how she viewed it. He probably was seeing someone else, and if he was Peyton couldn't blame him. She had been a poor wife and if someone else had pulled him, she could only blame herself.

Mrs. Garcia entered the family room pushing a cart with Peyton's food, which included a full course meal, dessert, and beverage.

"Mrs. Garcia, do you mind taking my food to my room? I don't feel like eating in this big room all by myself."

"Yes, Mrs. Hudson. Do you need help to get on the stair lift?

"Liam is here. Just send him back down here. He'll see to it that I get on it safely."

"I don't mind helping you, or I can get the nurse, if she's still here," Mrs. Garcia offered.

"The nurse has left for the evening."

"Liam is already upstairs, Mrs. Hudson. That boy is probably sitting in front of the television in his study eating like there's no tomorrow while watching that show he loves." Mrs. Garcia laughed.

Peyton smiled. "You're probably right. I'll meet you at the foot of the stairs," she said.

Mrs. Garcia watched as Peyton transferred herself to the stair lift. She pushed the button and it began taking her up the staircase where a manual wheelchair sat in the corner.

Mrs. Garcia hurried up the stairs to meet Peyton at the top of the stairs and pulled the second chair close enough where Peyton could transfer to it. Once she was seated, she rolled to her master bedroom.

There were seven bedrooms upstairs and five bathrooms. Derek slept in one of them at the other end of the hall. Liam had his own wing on the other side of the house with a study, game room, and a guest room for him and his friends when they came over.

Mrs. Garcia went back downstairs and returned with a tray of scrumptious food. Beef Wellington, risotto, and a green beans and asparagus casserole. Dessert was a slice of triple chocolate cake with sweet tea and a glass of water that accompanied the meal. It was far from the quick and easy meal she asked Mrs. Garcia to prepare, but Peyton was not complaining.

While Peyton dined alone, she read a chapter of one of the books she had started until she finished eating. Afterwards, she showered and got ready to relax for the night.

Peyton tossed and turned in the bed, unable to sleep or find the perfect position. She reached for the remote control next to the king-sized bed and pushed the button. A 65-inch television rose out of the foot of the bed. Peyton pushed the channel button and scrolled through the guide until she found one of the reality shows she watched from time to time.

Tears began to flow out of nowhere. She couldn't control herself. She was hurting, not physically but her heart hurt something terrible. She had ruined her life and everyone's life around her. Liam's biological mother, Breyonna, was dead, Carlton's marriage had been on shaky ground until lately, and her marriage was as dead as a pet rock.

She turned off the television and wept. She didn't hear anyone enter the room so she was startled when she heard Derek's voice.

"Peyton, what is it?" he asked as he sat down on the bed next to her. "Are you in pain? What can I do?" His voice sounded genuinely sympathetic.

Peyton refused to turn over and face him. She didn't want him to see her boo-hooing like a little baby. She didn't want his pity either—she wanted his love. She needed to be touched, made love to.

Somehow, Derek must have sensed her agony. He leaned over and grabbed her into his arms as he got in the bed next to her.

"It's going to be all right. It takes time," he said, holding on to her like he would never let her go.

Did he realize what he was doing?

"Stop it, Derek!" she screamed and pushed away from out of his arms.

He jumped back and Peyton turned toward him and looked into his seeking eyes. "You're only making it worse."

"What?" he asked. "Did I hurt you?"

"No, I'm not in pain. At least not that kind of pain. I've made a mess of everything," she cried. "Our marriage, our lives. My son barely speaks to me. You barely speak to me. No one wants to be around me. I can't walk. I've ruined it all. I'm just so sorry. I know I can never make it up to you, and I understand that. But it doesn't make it any better for me. I feel so alone. Drinking at least would numb these feelings."

Derek stiffened. She could tell he didn't like her talking about her alcohol addiction. "So that's what you want to do? You want a drink, Peyton? After everything you just said, you can still think about drinking when you know it's what ruined everything?"

"I can think about it and I probably always will, but I will never ever take another drink. I'll literally die before I do that. I'm just saying that it hurts like hell to be in this big ole room night after night, all alone, when my husband sleeps in the other room. It's hard to face the fact that you don't want or desire me anymore. I'm just, just tired of it all." Peyton began to weep again, this time almost uncontrollably.

Derek looked at his wife. She was still beautiful. She always had been. There were women out there who he thought about being with but somehow, he hadn't crossed that line. He had gotten awfully close but the fact remained that he hadn't, and he didn't want to. He wanted to honor his vows and his marriage. That was one thing that he was determined to do until God gave him direction about whether or not he would stay with her or whether he and Peyton would get a divorce.

He reached over to his left side and got a couple of tissues and wiped Peyton's tears. Then he used the back of his hand to wipe more of her tears as they fell like a waterfall from her beautiful blue green eyes.

He kissed the top of her head and inhaled the sweet fragrance of her freshly shampooed hair. She smelled divine and his urges overtook him as his manhood began to take over his thinking. His hands roamed over her body, taking in every curve, every mound, and the thickness of her. She was as soft as a satiny pillow and her scent drove him wild. The mixture of her salty tears with her sweet lips caused him to groan as his hands lifted her gown and explored her fully. He missed her. She didn't smell like alcohol and he was totally into her.

It wasn't pity that he felt; it was a mixture of his love for her and the loneliness he too felt from not making love in months. He needed her, longed for her. He heard moans escape from her like a guttural sound as he pulled back just long enough to get out of his clothes.

Peyton couldn't believe this was happening. Was this *her*

Derek? Was he removing his clothes and getting into bed with her? This was what she had wanted for so long. *God*, she said in her mind. *Thank you. Thank you.*

She lay back as Derek, naked as the day he was born, eased the covers back. "I want to see every inch of you," he whispered hungrily as he pulled her gown over her head, exposing her bare milky white skin.

He began kissing her from her lips to the sides of her neck. His kisses trailed the full length of her body as he devoured her. He lifted his head and looked down on her as he eased his body on top of hers.

Peyton could barely speak. "Derek," she said in a faint tone.

"Yes, Peyton."

"Derek," she said again.

"Yes…Peyton," he responded in his own sexual tone.

She met his every thrust as their bodies meshed. The timing was on point and nothing could take the place of this moment as they satisfied one another.

Chapter 6

"A tiger doesn't change its stripes but it will hide in tall grass so you don't notice them." Jae Henderson

Eva lay in the bed alone, missing Harper again. Tonight, he was at the television studio filming segments for his television show. She didn't know when he would make it home and when he did she already knew what he would do. He would maybe get a light bite to eat, take his shower, and then go to one of the rooms in the house where he would sleep.

If he didn't truly want her then why did he even ask her to come back home? Eva was fed up. But she had to stay in this marriage until she was able to make things happen on her own for her and her family. She couldn't ever go back to living the way she lived in Bolivia, and she couldn't subject her family to that kind of lifestyle again either.

School would be starting in a few days and she couldn't wait. She was going to pour herself into it totally and completely with a goal to finish school and open her own restaurant. Not only that, she would open several restaurants, maybe even one in Bolivia. She lay on the bed, closed her eyes, and dreamed of being happy once again like she was when she and Harper first met.

He had been the perfect man in her eyes, sweeping her off her feet and treating her like she was pure gold. How could she have fallen for Seth that night? Yes, she was lonely and she was desperate. A young woman like her had needs. Didn't Harper realize that? Surely, he had to know that she wanted children. They had talked about it, and he never once told her that he had a vasectomy. He only said he didn't want to have kids right away. He said he wanted them to enjoy being together, just the two of them, without kids being in the way. Eva was all for that. She understood that he wanted them to be free of kids in the beginning of their marriage so they could travel, enjoy getting to know one another, and having fun. After they had been married almost two years, she started talking to him about them having a child. Harper began to clam up. He spent more time at the hospital and less time at home. Their love life suffered tremendously and Harper became aloof. The only thing that hadn't changed was his desire to go to church whenever he could, and he expected her to attend with him.

Eva thought things would change when she took Avery's advice and stopped taking her birth control pills without telling Harper. She was ecstatic about not being on the pill, knowing that things would be perfect when they had a child running through the house…until she did the unthinkable and got pregnant.

The night she slept with Seth she was so lonely, felt so vulnerable, and Seth undoubtedly knew it. After all, he knew his father was never at home, never around. He'd said it to Eva more than once that his father had his sight on other things and not on her. She didn't want to believe him, but the night he grabbed her and kissed her she couldn't resist him. She wanted Harper to be the one kissing her so she closed her eyes and fantasized that it was Harper making love to her, holding her, caressing her over and over again, but it wasn't Harper. It was Seth, and she would regret what she did for the rest of her life.

She closed her eyes to sleep but was jarred awake with heaviness over her body. She slowly opened her eyes and saw Harper.

"Who was it?"

"Huh?" she said, confused.

"Tell me who it was," Harper insisted again, this time his voice sounded abrasive and raised.

As soon as she opened her eyes, he began kissing her. She felt his manhood against her. He began pounding her vigorously. She missed him, and she needed this so much—until each stroke became harder and harder to the point it began to hurt her. She couldn't fully enjoy the moment because of what he had said. Had he somehow found out about her and Seth? *God, no. Please don't let him know.*

"You were with my son! God hates adulterers and harlots!" His voice became more elevated and his thrusts harder.

"Wait, Harper, please. Let me explain," she said, trying to push him back but to no avail. "You're hurting me. *Por favor*, stop, hold up," she pleaded.

"Tell me! Tell me if you slept with my son, you harlot," he demanded.

She wanted him to stop. She was petrified. This wasn't the Harper she knew. She smelled the stink of alcohol on his breath. He was drunk, but Harper didn't drink, unless it was a cocktail or a glass of wine from time to time if he was in a social setting. This was different. She smelled hard liquor on his breath. It frightened her even more. She begged and pleaded.

"Tell me the truth!" he demanded, hurting her even more. "Tell me now!"

"Yes, yes it was Seth. It was Seth," she sobbed loudly. "Now, please…stop, Harper. Please."

Harper didn't seem to hear her. He continued with a harshness she'd never known or experienced before. Each of his thrusts felt like her body was being ripped apart. She tried to talk but he smothered her with hard, angry kisses. When she tried to push him away, he penned her arms down to her sides and continued pounding her with each of his loud grunts. It hurt so badly and tears rushed from Eva's eyes.

"This is what you want? This is how you want to be treated? You want to mess around on me?" he said angrily. "I'll teach you not to cheat on me," he said as his strokes caused her to scream but not in pleasure. He flipped her over and had his way with her in other ways she'd never before experienced. She couldn't move and he took her and used her for his own sick pleasure. When he was finally done, he laid spent beside her. She still couldn't escape his grip as he held her in his arms.

"Don't even think about leaving me. If you do, you'll regret it for the rest of your life," he said before he drifted off to sleep."

Eva's tears continued to trail heavily down her face, onto her neck, and onto the sweaty and soaked sheets. She didn't know when she fell asleep or even how she was able to fall asleep. Every part of her body ached. Was this what it had come to? She had a lot of growing up to do and whether he realized it or not, Harper had just taught her a crucial life lesson of survival.

Chapter 1

"All relationships go through hell. Real ones get through it."
Heartfelt quotes

Meesha woke up and sat up in the bed. She yawned slightly as she eyed the baby monitor. It was time for Makena's midnight feeding. She saw the newborn twisting and turning and then heard her tiny cry. Carlton didn't budge; he was too busy snoring.

Their little girl cried softly and Meesha got up, walked to the baby's nursery, and sat in the rocking chair after picking up Makena from her crib. She cradled her in her arms as she exposed her breast to feed her. She looked at her daughter with love and adoration.

"Thank you, God," Meesha whispered, looking slightly up toward the ceiling. She looked back down at the baby and smiled as the little girl suckled her breast.

Meesha was glad she had given her marriage another chance. She only hoped that things would truly work out between her and Carlton. She never quite understood why Carlton had begged, practically demanded, a divorce in the first place, but she tried to push it out of her mind. Whatever he had been going through she believed it had to do with Breyonna and the fact that he believed he was Liam's father. Now that Breyonna had met her tragic demise and Liam was found not to be Carlton's biological son, their lives returned to some semblance of normalcy. She didn't want a divorce in the first place, but she was willing to give Carlton one if that's what he wanted. She didn't want to be with anyone who didn't want her.

Her mind surprisingly drifted toward thoughts about Avery. She wondered how things were going with the new addition to Avery's family. She couldn't understand Avery's coolness toward her over the past months. She hadn't done anything to jeopardize their long friendship so she figured that Avery was going through some personal things that she didn't want to share. Avery had been known to suffer from bouts of depression so maybe it was depression that had caused her to treat her less than friendly lately. Her pregnancy probably had something to do with it, too. A woman's hormones could get totally out of whack when pregnant.

Meesha prayed that she wouldn't suffer from postpartum depression. She'd experienced it after the birth of her two youngest sons and it took her for a real loop. For a period of time after each of their births, she stopped eating, became depressed, and withdrawn. She had some weird thoughts and found it hard to care for her boys. Thank God Carlton recognized it and got her some help mentally and also brought help into the house in the form of their live-in nanny who was still with them.

God delivered her from her bouts with postpartum depression a few months after each of their births. She didn't want to ever experience that again, and definitely not with the precious little princess she held in her arms.

After Makena was done eating, Meesha burped her, changed her diaper, and held her while she herself drifted off to sleep sitting in the rocker. Right now, life couldn't be any better.

After little Ryker was born, Ryker presented Avery with names they could call him other than Ryker the Second or Ryker Junior. The names were R2 for Ryker the Second, or RJ for Ryker James since James was Ryker's middle name. Avery told him she preferred RJ. She didn't want her son being called R2 like he was a Star Wars characters. Ryker agreed, and they settled on calling him RJ.

Almost immediately, after RJ's birth, Avery began experiencing postpartum episodes. Identical to Meesha, Avery experienced a short but mild bout with postpartum depression after the birth of each of her girls, but this time it was worse.

Ryker was well aware of his wife's struggles, and immediately sought help in the form of the temporary live-in nanny and insisting that Avery start back with her weekly therapy sessions. He hoped that the depression would pass sooner rather than later, understanding that some women could be tormented with the mood disorder for years.

Having already had one failed suicide, he couldn't and wouldn't take the chance of her trying a repeat performance, or worse yet, doing something harmful to his children.

At the Mitchelson household, Avery tossed and turned as she looked over at Ryker soundly sleeping. Their son was lying between them because ever since they'd come home from the hospital, Ryker refused to let the baby sleep in the nursery or his crib.

They had a portable crib in their master bedroom next to their bed but that wasn't good enough for Ryker. He wanted RJ in the bed with them.

Avery looked at her sleeping son and at Ryker. Did he resemble Ryker or did he look more like Carlton? There was no mistaking about their girls. Ryker was their father because she had never cheated.

Eleven-year-old Lexie was the spitting image of Ryker with coffee bean brown skin, deep brown, doe shaped eyes and a head full of long black hair. Nine-year old Heather had features more like Avery's French Canadian mother and African American father. Heather's hair was more of a blondish brown. Her son could very well be Ryker's and then again, Avery couldn't tell. It looked like he had Ryker's thick eyebrows and his same skin tone, but his lips looked like Carlton's. She felt like she was one of the women on the Maury show talking about, "See he has his eyes, he has his upper lip, he has his ears." Was she that bad? *Probably so*, she thought.

Avery hoped that she hadn't made a mistake telling Eva about her and Ryker's recent marriage, her affair with Carlton, and her suspicions about who Little Ryker really belonged to. But Eva had been a good friend. Avery hadn't had a real friendship like that since she was in high school and was best friends with a girl named Joanna Webb. Joanna was dead now. Her husband, who was Joanna's high school sweetheart, killed her and then killed himself a few months after they walked down the aisle. It was such a sad and heartbreaking period.

Avery often thought about how she could have met a similar fate had she not gotten out of the call girl business. It was a tough and dangerous life she used to live. She was glad that part of her life was over and done. Ryker had been responsible for so much good in her life and yet here she was catching feelings for another man. He looked over her past and accepted her for who she was. Not once had he thrown it up in her face, at least not verbally. She often thought the reason he didn't marry her was because of her past, but now she could only smile at the thought that he had finally made good on his promise and made her his wife.

She got up out of their bed as quietly as possible, so as not to wake up Ryker and the baby. She picked up her cellphone which she kept mostly on Silent and then eased out of their bedroom and went downstairs to the kitchen.

She texted Carlton. She needed to talk to him or she would not be able to rest. Avery paced the floor as she texted. We need to talk. Are you awake? Several seconds passed, but she didn't get a response. She texted him again. I know it's late but we really need to talk. We have a lot of unfinished business. Still no reply. She then dialed his cell phone. It went straight to his voicemail. "Don't you dare try to play games with me, Carlton Porter," she said under her breath. "You should know by now that I'm not the one to be messed with or messed over," she seethed.

She dialed his phone again, each time getting herself worked up more and more. She texted him again. Maybe she really was a crazed woman, but to be ignored was one of the things she despised most in the world. Whenever Ryker ignored her, Avery would blow up and when she did, it wasn't a pretty sight. Carlton definitely didn't want her to go that route.

"If you knew what was good for you, you would answer me!" She began to talk out loud. Her voice grew louder.

"Avery, what are you doing? Who are you yelling at?" Ryker asked as he burst into the kitchen.

Avery, startled, turned around, looking wide-eyed at her husband.

"I… it was nothing. I just needed to talk. I was feeling a little low and I didn't want to wake you up, so I thought I'd call my sister, but she's not answering."

"Probably the time difference. You should get back to bed. You haven't talked to her in ages anyway. What's really going on?"

"Nothing, I'm fine. You go back upstairs and check on the baby. Don't leave him alone like that, especially in our bed. I don't like it."

"Just come on upstairs," Ryker said and almost demanded before he turned and walked out of the kitchen.

Avery cussed under her breath at the thought that Carlton hadn't answered. She hated the fact that she let him get under her skin the way he did. She didn't want to let him off the hook if RJ was his kid. She went back to her bedroom and climbed in the bed.

"You okay now?" Ryker asked.

"Yeah, sure," she said and turned over on her side. *You will pay, Carlton. If you want to do me this way, treat me like I'm yesterday's garbage, then revenge is what I want. Nothing but pure unadulterated revenge. And I will get it—somehow someway.* Avery turned back to face Ryker, placed her arm across little RJ and Ryker, and went straight to sleep.

Chapter 8

"The cunning man uses deceit, but the more cunning man shuns deception." Adam Ferguson

Carlton was awakened out of his sleep by the vibration of his cell phone. He was used to getting calls all times of night because of the large congregation he serviced, but it still wasn't the best feeling. He loved his sleep and lately, with the baby, he got less than usual. He turned in the bed and lazily, with sleep in the corner of his eyes, looked over and saw his phone on the night table. He reached for it and instantly grew angry. It was Avery. What in the world was she thinking? She had sent him at least ten text messages and he had four missed calls. The phone began to vibrate in his hand and this time he quickly answered.

"Are you out of your mind? Why are you calling me, and at this time of night! What do you want?

"We need to talk. It's time to tell Ryker and Meesha about us."

"What are you talking about? There *is* no us," Carlton said, shouting under his breath while looking over his shoulder to make sure Meesha didn't suddenly reappear. Was she in the bathroom or what? He got up and walked over to the other side of the bed and eyed the baby monitor. She was in the baby's room asleep in the rocker. She often fell asleep in the nursery after feeding Makena. He breathed a sign of welcomed relief.

"Look, lady, don't you ever call me at this time of night, or ever, with this nonsense. What we had is over. What in the world is it going to take to get that through your stupid head." He gritted his teeth and clenched his mouth as a cold knot formed in the pit of his belly. He walked back to his side of the bed and sat back down. His temples began to pound and his blood pressure must have certainly shot up.

"Look, I will not be brushed off, Carlton Porter. We need to settle things once and for all. Now tell me when you want to meet," Avery demanded.

"You know darn well that kid isn't mine! Now stop with the stupid antics. You had that baby at least two months before you told me it was due. I don't know what kind of lie you told the doctor and I don't know what game you're playing, but you got the wrong one. That kid is not mine, Avery!" He lay back in the bed still holding the phone in his hand, and prayed that none of this would blow up in his face.

Meesha stumbled into the room, holding her head. She couldn't believe the words she heard pouring out of Carlton's mouth.

Carlton turned around. His heart raced and sweat suddenly appeared on his forehead. "Meesha," he said, and dropped his cell phone onto the hardwood floor "I…."

"You dirty, filthy, lying dog," she screamed and rushed up to him and started pounding him with her small fists all over his body. Her nostrils flared with fury.

"How…could you?" She was so furious she could hardly speak. Suddenly, two of their boys burst into the room. Obviously they had heard the commotion.

"Mom, what's wrong?" CJ said and rushed up to his mother ready to defend her at all costs.

Son, it's all right," Carlton said. "Your mother just heard

some bad news. She's going to be okay. Let me get her settled. Go back to your room."

Meesha couldn't stop crying; she plopped down on the bed and then managed to look up at her two boys. "Please, do like your father says. I… I'm fine."

Yes, ma'am," the oldest one said. He touched his brother's shoulder and the two of them left back out of the bedroom.

"Close the door behind you," Carlton ordered and they did.

Meesha picked the phone up off the floor.

Avery was still on the other end and heard everything. *Serves him right*, she thought. *He should have listened to me, and did what I told him to do, but noooo he wanted to play these childish games. Well, this will let him know that I'm not the one to be played with. God don't like ugly.*

"Avery, Avery, are you there?" Meesha barked into the phone.

"I'm here," Avery answered in an eerily calm voice.

"So, this is the reason for your whole attitude change toward me. You've been smashing my husband? Is that his child you have over there?" Meesha was sickened at the thought. She looked back at Carlton and shot him a cold look of disdain.

"It's not like what you might think. Carlton loves me and I love him. We can't help that we fell in love. We were going to spend the rest of our lives together until you went and got yourself pregnant…again! Well, having another kid is not going to save your fake marriage, Meesha. You're yesterday's news and me and Carlton are going to raise our child together. You wait and see."

"You're one crazy heifer," screamed Meesha. "Don't you ever come anywhere near me or my family again or you'll be sorry," Meesha threw the phone as hard as she could across the room.

Carlton held his head with both hands as he walked back and forth. He was clearly shaken and didn't know how he could have messed up so royally. Why couldn't he see that Avery was unstable? He should have clearly seen it when she tried to commit suicide, but he was taken in by his own lust and now he was about to pay a price that his massive millions wouldn't be able to come close to covering.

"Carlton! Carlton!" Meesha called.

Carlton bolted upright in the bed, a bead of sweat on his brow. He looked around confused and dazed by his surroundings with Meesha standing over him. He looked at her strangely, waiting on her to tell him to get out, but instead she said something that caused him to close his eyes, inhale, and then exhale slowly with relief.

"Honey, what is it? You were practically yelling in your sleep. Are you all right?"

Carlton continued to look around their bedroom. "Yea, yea I'm fine. I guess I was dreaming."

"Sounded more like a nightmare rather than a dream," Meesha said while she walked back to her side of the bed, climbed back into the bed, and got underneath the bedcovers.

"Makena all right?" Carlton asked.

"Yes, I fed and changed her. See, she's sleeping like the beautiful little princess that she is," Meesha said, pointing at the baby monitor.

Carlton looked at his sleeping beauty, smiled, and thought. *Thank you, Lord.*

Chapter 9

"Chance favors only those who court her." Charles Nicolle

"You should know this won't change anything between us," Derek told Peyton after their steamy lovemaking. It was what we both needed but it can't erase the past or present circumstances in our marriage, Peyton. Too much has happened that's damaged us." He lay next to her on his side of the bed, head resting on his hand. He turned to look at her. His emotions were all over the place. He didn't want to give her false hope that making love would rectify all of their problems. Or was it himself that he was trying to convince? He always had a weak spot for Peyton, something he believed she knew and had taken advantage from the very first time they met. He was smitten by her beauty and her boldness. She exuded confidence and had a certain roughness about her that intrigued him. If there was a such thing as love at first sight, he felt it the moment he laid eyes on her. The little boy she introduced him to as her adopted son drew him to her even more. That little boy, Liam, was his heart. He longed for his own children, but even if he and Peyton had other children, it would not replace the love he had for Liam.

He listened as Peyton spoke. He could hear the hurt in her voice and inside he was sorry, but he was not going to retract his words.

"You made love to me only to tell me that nothing's changed? How could you be so cruel, Derek? I can't believe you would do something like this. What more do you want from me? How many times or ways can I tell you how sorry I am for everything I've done? Do you like seeing me suffer?" Peyton turned over in the bed away from Derek. "Just go, please. I don't need your sympathy. Just leave," she cried.

Derek arose from the bed and then paused and looked over his shoulder at his wife. He felt terrible for hurting her but he had his own heart to protect too. Women sometimes act like men can't be hurt and that a man's world is hard to shatter but Derek felt quite the opposite. He once loved Peyton with everything in him, but her words, her actions, and her drinking had stabbed his heart too many times to count and he refused to let himself be mortally wounded—again. Not by Peyton, not by anyone. His main concern now was raising Liam to be a good person and an even better man. He hadn't exactly made up his mind about leaving Peyton, and that was something that she was right about…it wasn't fair to her and he had to do something one way or the other.

As she stirred around the house the next morning, Peyton hoped that things with Derek would have had a different outcome after last night. To hear him tell her that nothing had changed caused another blow to her already delicate heart. She called for help to get downstairs and her personal assistant showed up in minutes and helped her to the staircase and the lift. Once downstairs, she rolled around, combing through every cabinet she could and every secret place she would normally have stashed liquor. She searched and searched but to no avail. There was not a drop of liquor in the house. She knew there wasn't but she hoped that maybe, just maybe, a bottle had been accidentally left behind.

After growing more frustrated, Peyton called Meesha. She needed to talk to someone before she called the package store and had vodka delivered to the house, and she didn't want it to be her counselor. She needed to hear the voice of a friend, a real friend. At the end of the day, Meesha was the one she trusted the most. Meesha would give her the best advice, listen to her without talking down at her, and sincerely lift her up in prayer. Peyton felt she needed prayer at this moment.

A still small voice told her not to call the package store. She had come too far. Her counselor would have told her that she had to be strong and learn how to face the disappointments, setbacks, and problems of life without turning to alcohol.

"Hey. Peyton. What's going on, girl?"

"I want a drink so bad, Meesha."

"Peyton, calm down. You can get through this. Did anything happen that has you wanting to jeopardize all you have accomplished for almost a year?"

"I thought Derek and I had turned a corner and had a chance at rekindling our marriage. I was wrong. I don't know how to deal with this." She swallowed hard and bit back tears.

"Wait, hold up. Slow down. Tell me what happened."

"Last night was magical between me and Derek. We made love for the first time in ages. He hadn't touched me like that, well in months, Meesha. Then afterward he turns around and tells me that it didn't change anything between us. I mean, how could he do that to me? How could he say that? And why would he even go there if he knew it meant nothing to him. That was just mean and cruel. I'm so tired of being used. I need a drink. Just one tiny drink to calm my nerves." She yielded to the tears that slowly found their way down her cheeks.

"Listen to me, Peyton. First of all, you do not need a drink. You can do this. As for Derek, that was wrong of him, but knowing Derek the way I do, and you should be able to vouch for this too, you know he is not the kind of guy that would do or say anything to intentionally hurt you. If the two of you made love it's because he wanted you, desired you. I mean put yourself in his shoes. He's been hurt by you just as much, if not more than, you've been hurt by him. He's probably afraid to put his whole heart out there and then you stomp on it again. I'm just being for real. I'm not going to tell you what you want to hear. I'm going to tell you the truth."

Peyton cried softly into the phone, but she listened to Meesha's every word. Maybe that's why God had placed Meesha into her spirit to call. She needed to hear the truth.

"Are you there?" Meesha asked after an extended silence over the phone.

"Yeah, I'm here. I was listening to what you said. It hurts so bad though, Meesha. I mean, everything was perfect last night. I just thought—"

"Look, now is not the time to go back to your old ways of coping with your disappointments by drinking. That would be proving Derek right. The man doesn't know if he can trust you just yet, Peyton. At the least sign of trouble you want to go back to drinking? No way. Get yourself together, girl. You're bigger and better than that. God has brought you too far for you to give it up all in a matter of minutes by trading it in for a drink."

"You're right; I could be dead," Peyton said, still crying. She looked around to make sure no one was around. She pushed the wheelchair button with her free hand and rolled up the long winding hallway until she got to their home study. She leaned over a bit to open the door and then pushed the button and rolled inside, closing the door behind her.

She rolled over to the huge picture window that displayed their beautiful garden. It was a peaceful spring day. The sun was beaming. She saw several birds flitting around the garden and even a few butterflies. Her tears continued and she used one hand to wipe her eyes before rolling over to the desk and opening one of the drawers to retrieve a box of tissue.

"Are you listening to me?" Meesha asked, concerned about her friend. Peyton could be brass, tacky, gossipy, and sometimes inconsiderate of others' feelings, but she was also a sensitive person who wore her heart on her sleeves. She felt bad that things hadn't turned out exactly as Peyton had hoped, but Peyton had to face the fact that she had hurt Derek, Liam, and well, no telling how many other people with her *I don't care about anyone but Peyton* attitude. She had her own money well before she met Derek, and she and her family had been instrumental in helping him rise to the top, but being the genius Derek was, when he sold his social media APP a few years after meeting Peyton, he made millions. He didn't need to work at Adverse City General Bank, he *wanted* to work there. He was the president of the company because he was a brilliant man. Yet, Peyton had belittled him all throughout their marriage. Sad to say, Meesha surmised that some of what Peyton was going through was payback. Yet, she didn't want to be the one to judge anyone. She left that up to God. She had her own secret demons, and could very easily be judged if others knew about her shameful past.

"Look, where are you? Are you in your bedroom? Are you alone in the house?"

"No, I'm downstairs in the study. Derek is gone to the office and Liam has already left for school. The housekeeper should be here and Beth, my personal assistant, is here. She's probably in the family room or kitchen. I'm sure the chef is here, too."

"Well, I want to say a prayer with you. Okay?" Meesha offered.

"Okay," Peyton cried.

"First, I want to tell you to let the tears fall. It's nothing wrong with crying. It's nothing wrong with that at all. Just know God sees you and he knows your pain and your situation. He has everything under his control, and I believe everything will work out for your good, but you have to be strong, Peyton. You have to fight against the enemy. He doesn't want you to be free from your addiction. He wants to keep you bound, but you have to take a stand against it. Do you hear me?"

"Yes, I hear you. I'm glad I called you, Meesha."

"I'm glad you called me, too. Now, let's pray about this." Meesha said a prayer over the phone. While she was praying she could still hear Peyton's whimpering, and her heart ached for her as she petitioned God for Peyton's healing mentally, physically and spiritually. She loved Peyton, Eva, and Avery. They had been her friends for a very long time. As she cried out to God on Peyton's behalf, she shed a tear too. "Amen," said Meesha and ended the prayer.

"Amen," Peyton said. "Thank you, Meesha. You're such a dear friend."

"You are going to be fine. You should feel good. Instead of calling the liquor store you called me. That's a huge step in the right direction. Give yourself some props for that. There was a time, and not too long ago, that you and I both know the choice you would have made. So you see, Peyton, you *are* growing. You're conquering this addiction one moment, one day at a time. I love you, girl."

"I love you too. Thank you sooo much. I don't know what I would have done. Oh, well, yes, I do. I would have done the unthinkable, thrown away every day that I've been sober all because things didn't go my way. I can't do that. I can't be so weak."

"You're definitely not weak, Peyton. Don't even go there. Applaud yourself. Celebrate yourself for making a wise choice. Rather than calling the package store, you called me. Praise God!"

Peyton heard Makena start crying. "Oh, well, I guess that's our cue. Sounds like Miss Makena wants some Mommy time," Peyton said, smiling instead of crying into the phone.

"Yep, it's about that time. She's ready to eat." Meesha laughed. "I'm glad you called, Peyton. Call me anytime you need to talk. Okay?"

"Okay, bye, Meesha."

Peyton remained sitting in front of the window for the next hour, staring out at the magnificence of the garden and the soft blue skies. She loved living in Adverse City. It was a fairy tale place. A place of luxury and splendor--the perfect place for her.

Thinking back on last night, she made a promise to herself. She was going to do everything she could to show Derek that she had changed. She was grateful for Meesha. She had helped to put things in perspective. Like the twelve step program that her counselor often referred to, Peyton had to ask for forgiveness to those she'd wronged and begin to live a different kind of life as a sober person. It was time for her to put her faith into action. She had no intent of becoming a religious zealot, but she did intend to pray more, seek God more, and treat people better, starting with Derek, Liam, and her friends.

Two sparrows came and perched on the ledge outside of the window. Peyton smiled. "I can do this. You're going to love me again, Derek Hudson."

Chapter 10

"Sometimes it's our secrets that define us." Britney Spears

Meesha looked down on Makena as the little girl nursed. She felt blessed to have such beautiful and precious children. Having a little girl was the icing on the cake and she was more than satisfied with the blessings God had chosen to bestow upon her and Carlton.

While Makena nursed, Meesha's thought transitioned from the present to her sordid past and the secret she bore—the one nobody but her and God knew about. Most times she could suppress the memories because of her active life. The children, her husband, her role at the Academy, and her friends, left her little time to think about the horrific deed she'd done. However, today was one of those days when it reared its ugly head. It was raining outside, the clouds were overcast, and it must have given the enemy the opening it needed to occupy her mind by bringing to the forefront that terrible night.

She was fourteen years old when she met and fell in love with Terrell Barnes. She and her family lived in Memphis, Tennessee at the time. Terrell was a junior in college from Virginia Beach, attending the University of Memphis and majoring in computer science. Yes, he was much older and a relationship like there's was forbidden. If her parents ever found out that she was seeing a boy in college, they would flip out. At that time Meesha didn't care. She was willing to take the chance because she loved Terrell, and she believed he loved her too because he told her that he did.

Terrell was her first boyfriend. No one paid much attention to her at school. She had lots of friends, but boys didn't seem to be attracted to her like they were attracted to her girlfriends. She didn't reason that she was only fourteen years old and she had plenty of time for boys.

One of her best friends during that time was a girl named Catherine. Catherine had one older brother and one younger sister. Meesha and Catherine would spend the night at each other's houses sometimes on the weekend.

Catherine's brother threw a small house party in celebration of his recent college acceptance. Catherine invited Meesha over to spend the night. When Catherine's parents went upstairs for the night, Meesha and Catherine changed their clothes and joined the party. Catherine's brother couldn't care less because he was too busy pushing up on his girlfriend who was now his wife.

Terrell approached Meesha that night and asked her for a dance. She felt all giddy inside as she looked back at Catherine. Terrell led her to the dance floor. He asked her all sorts of questions about herself and she gladly told him everything he wanted to know. He didn't tell her much about himself, only that he was in college and where he was from. They spent practically the rest of the night dancing and talking. Later that evening, as the party began to wind down, he took her by the hand and led her outside to his car. She knew that she shouldn't go with strangers, but Terrell was no stranger by this time, at least in her mind he wasn't. He was a boy who seemed really nice and he liked her. They sat outside in his car and she experienced her first kiss. It was magical! All types of funny feelings rushed through her young body. She felt a warm glow inside.

"You're beautiful, Sha. Can I call you that?" he asked as he pushed back a strand of her hair.

Meesha nodded, unable to get the word 'yes' out. She was mesmerized. The feelings going on inside of her were like none she'd ever felt.

"Okay, Sha it is. That's my special name for you because you're a special girl. I really like you. Do you like me?"

"Yea...yes," she stuttered.

"I want to see you again. Can I have your phone number, and I'll give you a call."

That night was the beginning of her relationship with Terrell. Terrell didn't care that she was fourteen years old. He said she was mature for her age, and soon Meesha had fallen in love.

They would sneak and see each other as much as they possibly could. It was good that Terrell had his own car because he and Meesha could arrange a place where he could pick her up without her parents or siblings knowing. There was only one person who knew about her and Terrell's secret relationship and that was Catherine. Meesha could trust Catherine not to say a word to anyone because Catherine was secretly seeing Terrell's friend and roommate named Cash. Sometimes when Meesha and Terrell hung out, Catherine and Cash would be somewhere doing their own thing, too. Terrell and Cash would occasionally sneak Meesha and Catherine into their dorm rooms.

"I love you, Sha," he told her one evening, less than a month from the time they met. "I hope you feel the same way about me. Do you?" he asked as they sat parked in a secret secluded spot Terrell often took her to.

"Yes, I do," Meesha confessed shyly. She loved Terrell more than anyone in the whole wide world.

"You're going to be my wife one day."

"For real, Terrell?"

"Yes, for real, baby. I want to show you how special you are, and I want you to do the same for me. You down with that?"

"Uh, sure. But what is it? How are we going to show each other?"

"You'll see." He started the car and drove off through downtown Memphis.

"Where are we going?" she asked as she cuddled next to him.

"It's a surprise."

He stopped at a liquor store and returned with a bottle of red wine.

"What's that for?" Meesha asked. She had never had a drink of alcohol in her life. Her parents were liberal Christians who enjoyed a glass of wine sometimes, but they forbid the children to even taste a drop. Catherine's parents would let her taste wine on holidays and even sometimes when it wasn't a holiday, but Meesha's parents were just the opposite.

"I told you. It's a surprise." Terrell flashed a smile at her, squeezed her thigh and leaned in and kissed her on the cheek. He continued driving until he drove into the parking lot of a small, dismal looking motel on Elvis Presley Boulevard. "I'll be right back," Terrell told her and went inside a door that had a sign over it that said "Motel Office."

Minutes later, he returned, showed her a key, and smiled again.

"Terrell," she said, smiling shyly. She trusted Terrell and had no worries.

He drove around the corner of the motel, parked and turned off the car. "Come on." He got the bottle of wine while Meesha, without putting up any protest, eased out of the car after him on the same side.

He took hold of her hand with his free hand, and they walked up to the door. He inserted the key and led her inside.

Meesha gave up her virginity that night, believing that when she graduated from high school and Terrell was done with college, that they would get married and live happily ever after.

Things quickly turned sour when she told Terrell that she

had missed two periods and that she might be pregnant. He was not happy at all. He showed a side that she had never seen before when he went into an uproar. They were downtown on Mud Island when she told him, parked in his car in a secluded section of the park that no one ever came to. It was where they always went when they wanted to be alone, and where they often engaged in sex.

"Who are you pregnant by?" he asked angrily as they stood in front of his midnight blue Chevy.

She couldn't believe it. Was he really questioning that he was the father? "Terrell, you know that I have never been with any other guy. I love you."

"You're lying. I don't even believe you were a virgin the first time we did it. I just didn't say anything, but this proves it."

"Terrell, please, don't say things like that. You know you were my first. I would never do such a thing."

Terrell wasn't having it. He began pushing and shoving her. "It's over between us! The best thing you can do if you are pregnant is to get an abortion," he screamed that night. "I don't want anything else to do with you. You're trying to ruin my life by tying me down with a brat. No way!"

Meesha began crying and couldn't stop. That only made Terrell angrier and he pushed her harder. He went out of control and began hitting and pounding on her. He knocked her to the ground and kicked her in her belly over and over again.

Seeing Terrell behave like this frightened her. She felt like she was about to pass out. Was he going to kill her? Somehow she had to stop him. She saw a brick lying next to her head. With a strength she didn't know she had, she picked it up and hit Terrell with it as hard as she could on the side of his head, knocking him backwards.

He fell to his back and Meesha immediately got up off of the ground. When Terrell barely stood to his wobbly feet, he lunged at her again, mouthing a stream of obscenities and cuss words. With heavy tears gushing from her eyes, she pounded him with the brick again. He feel backwards and on the ground. She continued hitting him until his flailing hands stopped and his stiff body lay bloody on the ground, eyes swollen and closed.

Meesha, crying hysterically, didn't know what to do. She looked around to see if there was anyone who could help her, but it was dark and they were out there all alone. Frightened and panicked, she threw the bloody brick into the Mississippi River. Next, still sobbing and hysterical, she ran to the car, reached inside the open passenger window, and grabbed hold of her purse before she took off running as fast as she could. She didn't stop until she made it to a nearby restaurant downtown. She dashed inside their bathroom, hoping no one saw her. Inside the bathroom stall, she sobbed some more, and then she vomited until she gagged.

What had happened? How could Terrell be so mean and cruel? What had she done? How could she leave him out there all alone? Maybe someone would find him and take him to a hospital, or maybe he would wake up and drive himself to the hospital. She cried until she couldn't cry any longer and then she set out on the long walk home.

The following day, Meesha heard nothing from Terrell. She wanted to return to their secret place so badly, but she didn't have a way, and she wasn't going to take that long walk again. There was no one she felt she could confide in, not even Catherine. She prayed to God that Terrell had woke up and returned to his dorm. After all, she couldn't have hit him that hard. She told herself that she had knocked him out and he was probably at his dorm, still angry with her, but okay.

Two days after that horrible, terrifying night, Catherine asked Meesha about Terrell.

"Have you heard from Terrell?" Catherine asked as they walked down the school hallway toward the cafeteria.

"No, he said he was going home to visit his family and that

he would call me if he got a chance, but he hasn't yet. I'm sure he'll call me though," Meesha lied. She was surprised that she was able to come up with a lie so quickly. "Why? What's up? Why are you asking about my man?" Meesha teased, trying to sound as normal as possible.

"Because Cash says he hasn't seen or heard from him in a couple of days. He didn't tell Cash that he was going home. Oh well, that's on those two," Catherine said, shrugged her shoulders, and the girls continued to the cafeteria.

When Meesha got home from school that afternoon, she saw her father standing with folded arms in front of the mounted television in the family room. "Hi, Daddy," she said.

"Hi, sweetie. What a shame. I don't know what this world or this city is coming to," he said, shaking his head from side to side in disgust.

Meesha was about to go to her room when she heard the name "Terrell Barnes." She walked slowly into the family room and stood next to her father and watched the news alongside him. That's when she learned that her worst nightmare had come true—Terrell was dead and she had killed him. She rushed out of the room and into her bedroom, quickly closing the door behind her. She fell on the bed and sobbed uncontrollably. From the time she heard the devastating news, she cried. She cried before school, after school. She even cried at school in the girls' bathroom stall. Catherine tried to console her but there was nothing she could do or say to make Meesha feel better.

No one knew of her and Terrell's plans to meet up that night, not even Catherine and Cash, and that turned out to be lifesaving for Meesha. Had Catherine or Cash known about it, they would be treating her in an entirely different manner, and Meesha most likely would be behind bars.

Catherine told Meesha that the police had gone to the university and questioned some of Terrell's friends, the professors, and anyone they thought might be able to tell them anything. Being his roommate, they questioned Cash to see what he knew, if anything, about Terrell. Thank God, Cash didn't mention her name as being Terrell's girlfriend. Meesha didn't know if it was because the police didn't ask or if Cash just didn't give her name because he knew that he and Terrell had both been dating underage girls. Whatever the reason, Meesha was relieved.

The news stated that a couple walking in the area found Terrell's lifeless body. Police determined that he was murdered in a mostly secluded area close to the muddy Mississippi shore. Meesha remained in shock that she was a murderer. Three days after she murdered the love of her life, her cycle started. She hadn't been pregnant after all.

One week after finding Terrell's body, police arrested and charged a vagrant with his murder. He had been caught shoplifting food out of a corner store. The store clerk detained him and called the police. When police searched the vagrant, they found Terrell's wallet in the man's pocket. He also had on the tennis shoes and socks Terrell had on that night. Terrell's DNA was all over the man.

Still silently grieving, distraught, and scared out of her mind, Meesha felt somewhat relieved when her family, due to her father securing a better job, had to relocate to Florida three months later. To this day, only Meesha and God knew who was really responsible for Terrell's death. No one could ever know what had happened that night, and she prayed daily that no one ever would. To this very day, her prayers had been answered. Was it God who answered her prayer or was the devil simply biding his time?

Meesha often replayed that ghastly night in her mind. Whenever she thought about the crime she'd committed in secret, she would beg God to forgive her and to be with the man who was serving time in jail for a crime that he had not committed. If that wasn't enough to drive a person to drink or do drugs, then Meesha didn't know what was. Instead, she turned to God and promised him that she would be the best Christian ever if only he would help her keep her secret.

She pushed the thoughts of that night out of her mind like she'd done for the past twenty-one years and continued to feed her sweet little Makena.

Chapter 11

"It hurts the most when the person that made you feel so special yesterday, makes you feel so unwanted today."
Unknown

The sun would be rising in a couple hours, and she had very little sleep. Eva looked next to her and saw Harper was still in the bed, snoring lightly. She took the opportunity to ease out of the bed with tears gathering in the corners of her eyes as she replayed the night's events. She crept to the bathroom, so as not to wake him, closing the door behind her. She turned on the shower and got underneath its hot, steaming jets of water. She showered until the water turned from toasty hot to freezing cold. No matter how hard she scrubbed, she couldn't wipe away the vileness of what her husband had done. She cried and her tears mixed in with the streams of water. She looked down and saw the last remnants of caked blood going down the shower drain. Harper had been cruel, mean, and abusive. He couldn't love her, not if he could violate her the way that he had. How could she ever trust or love him again?

You're a big girl, she heard a voice in her head say. *You can handle this. It's not like you haven't experienced being violated before. Remember those two men who attacked you and tried to rape you, when you were a young teen girl? You got away before they were able to sexually assault you. You've never told a soul about that and yet you pushed past that scary time, even when you saw them again. You will survive this too. Get whatever you can from Harper. Get it all. Use him to provide for your family and for yourself until you can finish school and open your own restaurant. You can do this,* the voice reassured her. *You…can… do…this…* Eva didn't know if she could though. The voice in her head fed her one thing, but her heart along with her bruised, sore, and aching body fed her something totally different.

When she stepped out of the shower, much to her relief, Harper was gone, which was no surprise. How had he found out about her and Seth? It had to have been Seth who told him, but why? Why would Seth do such a thing? Then again, she didn't know anything about Seth other than he was his father's college dropout son. She told herself that she deserved all of what had happened. She should have been more cautious, stronger, rather than give in to her flesh. When would she ever learn? Now she had paid a huge price for her infidelity and it appeared that the end of her torment might be nowhere in sight.

She pulled the sweaty, blood stained covers from off the king bed and then went to the huge linen closet on the other side of the bathroom where she retrieved a set of clean sheets before having second thoughts. She couldn't sleep in that room, and she didn't know when she would be able to sleep in it again. She turned around and went back to the room, and quickly dressed. She flipped through her phone and then called a number she had stored in her Contacts.

Next, she went to her walk-in closet and packed several items of clothing in an overnight bag before grabbing her purse, keys, and cell phone. She rushed out of the room, constantly looking around like she was a thief in the night. She ran to the bedroom where she kept her dogs whenever they weren't sleeping with her. She placed all three of them in the slightly oversized kennel that assured they had room enough to move around. With the kennel in one hand and the other items in the other, she raced down the stairs but as quiet as a mouse. She didn't stop to say good morning to Marissa. She hurried until she reached the entrance to the garage. She opened the door, stepped into the garage, pushed the FOB for her car, and rushed over to it, bypassing Harper's Land Rover, his Infinity, and his Corvette before reaching her car. Opening the door, she placed the kennel on the back seat, jumped inside the car, and pushed the garage remote. As soon as the garage door opened, she put the car in Reverse and sped out of the driveway, down the winding road leading out of their gated community and onto the main street.

Eva drove blindly with tears falling down her face as thought after thought poured through her mind. She drove along the interstate bypassing the majestic beach line. She didn't stop until she arrived at the Setai Hotel. She had reserved the suite when she got out of the shower. Being here would give her some time to think. This was the same hotel where she'd stayed when Harper threw her out of the house after she told him she was pregnant. Only this time, she was here by her own free choice. Harper had an open account with the hotel and Eva planned to take full advantage of it. For how long, she didn't know.

Once she arrived at the hotel, she gave them her name at the front desk, and was given the key to her suite. She left the front desk and walked along the marbled floors of the exquisite hotel until she arrived at Pet Concierge. They immediately removed the kennel with the frisky little dogs inside from her hand.

"Please take them for a walk and feed them too," she said politely. She hadn't allowed them to relieve themselves or eat because she was in a race to get out of that house. "I didn't bring their food. I was in somewhat of a hurry," she further explained.

"No problem, Mrs. uhhh,"

"Stenberg," Eva said.

"Yes, Mrs. Stenberg," the Concierge repeated. "It's always good to have you," he added.

"Thank you. Will you bring them to my suite when you're done? You can get my suite number from the front desk."

"Certainly, Mrs. Stenberg. And yes, your information is in our system."

Eva knelt down in front of the kennel and mouthed sweet words to her pooches before she stood upright and dashed toward the elevators.

After entering her suite, Eva undressed and took another hot shower. When she was done with her shower, she made herself a stiff drink from the fully stocked bar. She rarely drank hard liquor, but considering what she had experienced the night before, she felt that only a shot or two or three of liquor could wash away some of her physical and emotional pain.

She went outside and sat on the luxurious balcony of her hotel suite and stared out at the beach, drink in hand. The warm brown liquor and the beauty of the Adverse City skies and the ocean calmed her. A weird sense of peace overtook her. She would make it through this. She didn't want to consider the alternate choice.

Chapter 12

"One day I'm gonna hurt you—I promise." Unknown

Eva remained at the Setai for three nights before returning to her home and to her defiled bed. Harper hadn't called once while she was away, but knowing him with his vast array of connections, she guessed that he knew exactly where she was spending her nights. Not to mention that her stay at the Setai was on his dime, but Eva couldn't care less. She welcomed the time away from home, but back to reality.

When she returned home, she said as little as possible to Harper. He made that quite easy because like always, he was rarely at home. If he wasn't at the hospital, he was at the television studio and other off-site locations filming *The Heart of the Matter*. If he wasn't there, he was traveling around the country promoting his new book that bore the same title.

It was a relief for Eva because when Harper was at home, he pretended to be a sweet, loving husband, acting as if nothing had ever happened. Eva knew differently because she had experienced the flip side of his personality.

One evening, after being out of town for several days

promoting his new book, Harper approached her with three dozen long stem roses. They were absolutely beautiful. She was curled up in the family room on the huge wraparound sofa with her dogs lying next to her watching a movie when he walked in with the massive vase of flowers. She sat amazed, and took a quick breath in utter astonishment.

He walked up to her and placed the heavy vase of flowers on the table in front of the sofa where she sat. "For you," he said, his voice tender, and his tone apologetic.

Eva felt her heart melt the tiniest bit, but her tone didn't reveal that. "Thanks, they're lovely," she said as she leaned over and inhaled their sweet fragrance. "What's the occasion? Did I miss something?" she said dryly.

"No, it's no special occasion, but I do have some things I want to say. I hope you'll hear me out."

"Go for it," Eva replied, reaching for the remote and hitting the Mute button before crossing her arms and looking up at him.

Harper kneeled down in front of her and went full fledge into his spiel. He begged and pleaded for her forgiveness, told her how ashamed he had been of himself and that he had broken down when out of the blue, his own son had called him demanding money for his drug habit. Eva was unaware that Seth was on drugs, and Harper said he only found out about his son's addiction the night Seth called high and begging for money. Seth's mother called moments later and told Harper about their son's drug problem. Harper was devastated.

Harper further explained that Seth continued calling but Harper said he remained steadfast. He was not going to send him a dime. He told Seth the only money he would give him would be to pay for him to go into Rehab. Seth laughed and then things turned ugly.

Eva listened and stared wordlessly as she remained seated in front of him, her heart pounding.

"That's when Seth told me that he had slept with you," Harper explained. "That night, after hearing that the woman I loved, the woman I adored, had cheated on me with my own son, I lost it, Eva. I went to a bar after leaving the hospital and drank until I was inebriated. By the time I arrived home, my anger and hurt had reached an all-time high and that's when things took an ugly turn. And I can only tell you that I'm sorry, Eva. I'm sooo…so sorry for everything."

Eva told herself that it was still no justification for Harper to do her the way he did that night, but she could also understand how a person could go from zero to one hundred after learning that the people you loved had betrayed you.

"I don't know what to say. You hurt me, Harper. I've never known you to be such a cruel man. I don't know how I can get pass this."

"I know you're going to need time. I'll give you all the time that you need. Just tell me that you'll forgive me, baby. I've asked God to forgive me and now I need to know that you will at least try to understand how I was feeling."

She fought to control her swirling emotions. When he reached out and gingerly caressed the side of her face with the back of his hand, she lowered her gaze in confusion.

He lifted her chin and their eyes connected. She was entranced by the silent sadness on his face. When he leaned in and kissed her, she didn't object—his nearness made her senses spin as she gave in to the warmth and strength of his flesh.

Eva immersed herself into culinary school. She often enjoyed watching Marissa prepare various divine dishes, but now she was learning more than she ever imagined. She was eager to awake each morning and go to school. It was a different life for her, one that helped her maintain her sanity.

I want you to be a guest on the show, Harper texted one afternoon out of the blue.

"Me? Why would he want me to be a guest on his show?" Eva asked herself as she set her pecan Birkin bag on the table in the family room. She had just entered the house after coming from ladies' day out with the housewives.

`Why me?` she texted back.

`I want you to talk about foods and dishes good for the heart. Dishes from your native Bolivia that could be healthy. You are my wife, remember? Your family would be proud of you I'm sure.`

Eva understood what he was alluding to when he mentioned her family. She felt she had no choice but to tell him that she would do it.

The night before her scheduled appearance, Harper had been exceptionally kind. He insisted on taking her out to dinner at one of her favorite eating spots. Afterwards, he took her for a midnight stroll along Pointe Beach. It may have sounded foolish if she had told the housewives about his abuse, but being with him felt right. She had all but dismissed what had happened weeks prior because Harper was almost like the old Harper. She still loved him in spite of what he had done. She made excuses for him, telling herself that he was drunk and hurt at discovering she had slept with Seth.

When Harper reached for her hand as they walked along the beach, she welcomed it. The ocean waves kissed their bare feet and slowly she relaxed in his arms. This was the Harper she'd come to love. This was the Harper she couldn't seem to shake.

After they arrived home, the inevitable happened but this time it was sweet, tender, and passionate as Harper caressed her, kissed her hungrily, and told her over and over again how much he loved her.

She melted into his arms. When thoughts of the night he assaulted her tried to come to the forefront of her mind, she quickly pushed them back as he took her to pleasurable heights. She was sick all right, sick for *this* Harper. *This* Harper who cried for days after she returned home from the hotel. This Harper who told her how sorry he was for what he had done.

The day of the show, Eva rushed to the studio after she was done with culinary class. The housewives were going to be there for support and because they were eager to be a part of the studio audience.

Eva had chosen three heart friendly meals that were quick and easy to prepare, even for the novice cook. She had to admit that there was a part of her that was quite excited about appearing on Harper's TV show.

On the day of the filming everything went without a hitch. The dishes Eva prepared and showed how anyone could easily make at home, went off without a hitch. Harper doted on his wife and the housewives tried to clap louder than anyone else in the audience.

Was she a fool for asking God to give her the strength and mindset to forgive Harper? Maybe she was. But she wasn't perfect either. She entered the marriage knowing that she was not completely in love with him. She loved Harper as a person because he was good and kind. He helped save many lives when he came to Bolivia and performed heart surgery on the destitute—people who would not have a chance at living a full life had it not been for *Doctors Without Borders.*

When he wined and dined her while he was there, he swept her off her feet, but it wasn't enough to make her fall in love him completely. The man who had her heart at that time, the only man she had ever loved, was a poor Bolivian man named Juan Carlos. But Harper could offer her and her family what Juan never would be able to offer—a life of financial freedom, wealth, and a chance for their daughter, Eva, to prosper in America. She could not turn him down. She said goodbye to her family, ended things with Juan Carlos, leaving him brokenhearted and left with

Harper to start a new life in America.

It was like a fairy tale come true for Eva because Harper treated her like she was a queen. It was easy to fall in love with him, and soon she did, but she would never love him the way she loved Juan Carlos.

Her family told her recently that Juan Carlos had been approved for a K-1 Visa and would be moving to the United States to marry a nice lady he too had met, and fallen in love with. Eva hoped he would be happy and have a chance to live a good life.

That evening, after filming the TV segment, Eva and Harper enjoyed a relaxing dinner at home outside on their lanai. It was another enchanting night in Adverse City. They chatted lightly about the success of the show. Everything was beautiful until Harper's cell phone rang—it was Seth.

Seth and Harper argued back and forth until Harper abruptly ended the call. He looked over at Eva and went into a cursing rant toward her. He stormed over to their outside bar, took out a shot glass, and began to pour and drink, pour and drink, until he was drunk again.

"Harper, don't let him drive you to do this. You're better than this," Eva told him. "He's the one with the problem, not you."

"Who are you to give me advice about my son? All you know about him is how to sleep with him!"

"How many times do I have to say that I'm sorry, Harper? Let's not go there again."

To Harper what she said was nothing more than empty words from a woman whom he had given his whole heart to only to have it crushed. He turned a deaf ear to her words that turned into pleas. What started out as a wonderful evening outside underneath the stars turned into an encore performance of what had occurred weeks prior.

She has to pay, Harper thought. He thought of the passage of scripture about revenge. *Get rid of all bitterness, rage and anger, brawling and slander, along with every form of malice.* That's exactly what Harper intended to do—just not in the way God intended.

Chapter 13

"The best revenge is just moving on and getting over it.
Don't give someone the satisfaction of watching you suffer."
Unknown

Eva gathered her thoughts and tried to clear her mind of what had happened again between her and Harper a week ago this very day. She took the dogs for their morning stroll and relived everything that had gotten her here. She had been stupid to even believe in the first place that he was sorry for abusing her, but she so wanted to believe that it was a one-time thing. Part of her felt she was to blame because of sleeping with Seth. *All of this is your fault. You brought this on yourself,* repeated the voice inside her head.

When she returned home, she showered, got dressed, and went into the kitchen to tell Marissa that she was leaving for school.

"Senora, you fine?" Marissa asked, looking at Eva strangely.

"Yes, Marissa. Why do you ask?"

"I hear things. I see things," she said. "You must not anger Senor Stenberg. *Por favor.* I do not want you hurt."

They exchanged dialogue in their native tongue. Eva never imagined that Marissa had heard what happened between her and Harper. The house was huge and Marissa resided in the west wing of the house, far away from her and Harper's bedroom.

"What are you talking about, Marissa?"

"I see him…Senor Stenberg. He was very angry and said many not so nice things to you. You should not have done that."

"Done what?" asked Eva.

"With his son. That was wrong, senora. Very wrong."

Eva quickly turned her gaze away from Marissa out of embarrassment. She did not want Marissa to think bad of her or to know her business, but it seemed a little too late for that. "What else did you hear…and see?"

"That is enough to see," Marissa said, and began placing vegetables in a pot. "No need to see more." She added other ingredients and spices to the mixture.

"I'm sorry you heard what you heard, and yes, I am sorry for what I did. Please, do not say anything to anyone," Eva pleaded.

"Never, senora." Marissa shook her head vigorously from side to side. "Never do that," she further emphasized. She walked up to Eva, embraced her, and then like a mother would do, she pulled back, pointed her finger at Eva and said, "No more, but do not take more from him if he is too mean to you. You made a mistake and it is over," she said in Spanish, and kissed Eva on the cheek.

"Gracias," Eva said and kissed Marissa back on her cheek. "I should be home by three. I'm going to learn to cook as good as you." Eva grinned then reached down and patted each one of her barking dogs on the head as they gathered around her ankles.

"Quiet," she told the dogs. "Mommy has to go to school," she said, talking to the dogs like they were little humans instead of Yorkies.

"Si," Marissa said and smiled. "You will do fine with the cooking."

"I hope so, Marissa. I have to make it in this school." *If I don't, Harper can throw me out on the street and I will have nothing.* She made the thirty minute drive to the school and drove around the lot until she happened upon an available parking space.

Before exiting the car, she looked in her rearview mirror to study herself. She wanted to make sure she looked presentable. "Should I put my purse in the trunk?" she asked herself, then answered her own question by picking up the purse from off the seat beside her and getting out of the car, taking it with her.

Parking was not the best because this was a high-end area with some of the best of the best boutiques and restaurants. She and the girls had dined at a couple of them on their ladies' day out adventures.

As she walked toward the front door of the school, which was several doors down from where she parked, she began to feel a growing excitement at the new adventures she was about to face.

The loud bark of a dog from behind frightened her and Eva turned around. She'd seen that dog or one like it some time ago in the park not far from her community.

When she saw the face at the other end of the dog leash, she thought she recognized him as well.

The dog barked louder and louder and strained against the man's leash like he was trying to attack her.

"Keep that dog away!" Eva warned and quickened her pace.

"Don't worry, he won't bite. He likes you. He's not barking in anger."

"I have dogs. I know when they're barking in anger and when they're ready to attack. You keep him away!" Eva practically ran until she arrived at the entrance to the school. She loved dogs but only the small ones like her three little fur babies. Dogs this big were just not her forte.

She looked back and saw the man laughing. Someone exiting the building held the door open for her as she gave the man one last nasty stare before she paraded inside.

The day passed swiftly. The other six students were quite nice and the instructors were equally as nice and knowledgeable.

Eva and the group of aspiring chefs spent the day being

introduced to the program and the requirements. After giving it much thought, and in light of her home situation, Eva had made the decision to study Restaurant and Culinary Management in addition to the Culinary Arts program. If she was going to be the best she had to learn everything she could about restaurant management and becoming a chef.

At the end of class, she walked out with two of the students. She noticed the sign at the end of the block across from where she had parked.

Scooby Doo's Pet Accessories and Animal Rescue Shelter. Um, an odd location for a rescue shelter. She had never seen it before. It had to be a new establishment.

That must be where that monstrosity of a dog came from. Reading the sign again she swiftly crossed the street and stopped in front of the store. She peaked inside, thinking about the poor animals. She loved her dogs and she couldn't fathom anyone abusing or mistreating them or any other animals. The store looked more like one of the fashion boutiques she and the housewives frequented. It had lavish furnishings and from what she could tell, unique looking gifts inside.

As she curiously peered through the picture window she saw a Pomeranian dog relaxing on a chaise lounge, a Siamese cat strolling casually across the hardwood floor of the store, and the Scooby Doo dog sprawled along the floor on a large plush rug. *High class for sure,* she thought. The person who she assumed was the owner or an employee, was chattering away with a striking brunette who seemed to be giggling a little too much at whatever the man was saying.

Eva continued to look inside but did not think she was staring, when it dawned on her where she had seen the tall, handsome, stranger before. It was at Central Park. The same park she'd seen the lookalike dog. It was the *same* man and dog that she'd seen that day. That was so long ago, almost a year ago in fact, but the longer she stared inside at the stranger, the more she was sure it was him. She wanted to turn and leave, go get in her car, and go home, but something willed her to stay. Eva continued watching the exchange between him and the girl.

Eva stood to the side of the store, so it wouldn't appear that she was staring directly inside the shop as she began to recall that day she first saw him with astute clarity.

She was walking her Yorkies and listening to some Bolivian tunes on her iPhone. Without prompting, her dogs began barking ferociously. Eva saw a dog almost her height approaching her. It appeared to be a Weimaraner, usually a gentle dog, but her dogs could aggravate the most gentle of dogs…and humans. They jumped up and down, tugged against their leashes, and Eva almost fell to the ground when one of her legs became entangled in one of the leashes.

The owner of the Scooby-Doo sized dog rushed to her aid. It was the same guy that she'd seen today. She was sure of it. He was the one who helped her that day, keeping her from falling down, not one time but twice! She recalled how polite he was, and he was definitely quite easy on the eyes. When she almost fell down two times she recalled how embarrassed she felt. After helping her he asked if she was all right and she assured him that she was. She walked over to a nearby bench with her dogs and sat down, still trying to shake off her feeling of embarrassment. She wasn't expecting him to follow her, but he did. That's when he extended his hand and introduced himself. Eva tried to recall what he said his name was but she couldn't remember. That was a long time ago. What further confirmed that this was the same guy today was his slight accent. From what she'd remembered he sounded like he was from the New England states or maybe he had lived overseas. She didn't know. The guy today not only had the same familiar accent, but he also had the same bronze complexion, coal black hair, teeth that revealed he had a doggone good orthodontist and a body that made it evident that he enjoyed working out. Seeing him again, he wore that same, charming smile as Eva watched him through the window talking to the girl.

When someone walked past Eva and opened the door to the store, the handsome man looked up. Their eyes locked momentarily. Eva dashed out of his view and when she did, she tripped and fell to her knees.

She hurriedly looked around to see if anyone was watching before she got up and jetted across the street. A blaring horn jarred her even more, as she dodged the vehicle, ran to the parking lot, and got inside her car.

"Whew," she heavily exhaled with both hands planted firmly on the steering wheel. "How could you be so clumsy and stupid?" she chastised herself. "Ahhh," she screamed, startled when she heard a tap against her car window.

Looking up, it was *him*. She could feel herself turning a shade darker. "Uhhhh, yes?" she said without turning on the ignition and letting down the window.

"Are you okay?"

He was so daggone fine, even finer than she remembered him being in the park. Maybe this wasn't the same guy after all.

Eva nodded nervously. Why did he have such an effect on her? She'd seen good-looking, debonair, and suave men before. Harper was one of them, and she didn't recall reacting the way she was doing now or the way she did that day in the park.

She put the key in the ignition, starting the car, and pushed the button to let down the window.

"Uhhh, thanks, I'm good. I was...I didn't...I haven't. Uh, I mean this is the first time I've seen that pet store and rescue shelter. I assume that it's new?"

"Yes. Today is our grand opening. See the sign?"

She looked out of the window of her car and looked across the street. GRAND OPENING. The sign was right there on the entrance big as day. How had she missed it?

"You like animals?" he asked.

"Uh, yes."

He obviously didn't remember her from the park, and she asked herself, *why would he*? She was just a random stranger walking her dogs in the park that day. No need for him to remember her…like she remembered him. But she told herself she only remembered him because of his huge dog.

"You should visit the store and shelter," he suggested while flashing his hypnotic smile her way

"I'm sure I will, but not today. Nice talking to you." Eva put the car in Reverse, and eased out of the parking space while Mr. Scooby-doo stepped back, smiled, and waved as she drove off.

Chapter 14

"Though no one can go back and make a brand new start,
anyone can start from now and make a brand new ending."
Carl Bard

Derek accompanied Peyton to her orthopedic appointment, something he had been doing since she was involved in the drunk driving car accident that injured two police officers and caused her fractured ankles. Their marriage may have been on shaky ground but one thing she couldn't complain about was Derek's concern for her recovery. Whatever he could do to make her comfortable, he did. Every doctor's appointment she had, he was by her side. It was one of the reasons she found it hard to believe that Derek still wanted a divorce. And then there was the night they made love. Sure, weeks had passed since that night, but it was a night she would remember for a long time to come. There was no faking his passion and his desire for her.

"Mrs. Hudson, you will be pleased to know that your x-rays look remarkable. It shows your ankles have healed to the point that you can begin placing weight on your legs."

"Oh, Derek!" She reached next to her where Derek stood and grabbed hold of his neck. He smiled and gave her a big bear hug as he lifted her bottom off the table.

"You'll still need to wear mobilizers on each leg, and I don't want you going full speed ahead on your ankles. They're still somewhat weak. We'll continue with physical therapy to strengthen them. That will help you tremendously."

"Thank you, Doctor Moore. Thank you so much," she exclaimed.

"You've come a long way, Mrs. Hudson. Your healing process has been nothing short of miraculous. I want to see you back in my office in four weeks and we'll see how you're doing then."

Peyton was ecstatic. They waited in the doctor's office for another thirty minutes so Peyton could be fitted with new mobilizers and given a pair of crutches to assist her as needed.

She rolled out of the doctor's office, eager to start walking. "Wait until the ladies here this!" she said to Derek as they rolled outside and into the perfect day. The sun was shining, the temperature hovered at 70 degrees, and there was a light breeze.

They approached the car and Derek opened the door for Peyton to get inside. She stood up with a big grin encasing her cherub face.

He folded the manual wheelchair and put it in the back of his SUV, one of three vehicles they owned.

"Where to now?" he asked when he got in the car and turned the ignition.

"Hey, why don't you let me treat you to lunch?" she offered, looking at him and reaching out to touch the back of his hand gingerly.

He put the car in Reverse and backed out of the parking space. "I don't know. I need to get back to the bank."

"But it's close to lunch time. You have to eat, *aaand* you *are* the President of the bank. I don't think anyone will complain if you stop to eat after having taken your wife to her doctor's appointment." The tone of her voice was soft and resonated calm. She kneaded his hand that rested on the center console of the SUV. He didn't pull away. She didn't even sense objection to her touch. A good sign.

"So what do you say? We can go to Gianni's."

"We're not dressed appropriately for Gianni's, Babe."

Did he just call her Babe? His pet name for her? He did. Peyton smiled even bigger this time. "Derek, for goodness sakes. You have on a suit. And me, I think I'm more than dressed for Gianni's." She looked at her stylish dress. "Okay, forget Gianni's. What about MiaBea. It's eclectic, laid back, and you don't have to dress a certain way."

Derek stopped at the traffic light and looked at his wife. "You're not going to let me say no, are you?"

"Nope. I'm too excited about my doctor's report. I want to celebrate, and I can't think of anyone I'd rather celebrate with than you…well, of course, Liam, but hey, he's at school, so come on, let's do this."

The light turned green and Derek made a left turn, the direction of MiaBea instead of a right turn that would lead to their prestigious community. He drove down Adverse Boulevard, made the additional turns and twelve minutes later, he and Peyton were turning into the parking lot of MiaBea.

This day couldn't get any better for Peyton. Derek pulled into a vacant handicap parking space, and pulled out Peyton's temporary handicap placard and hung it on the rearview mirror.

"I want to walk inside, Derek," she told him before he got out of the car to get her wheelchair.

"Are you sure? Dr. Moore said he wanted you to take it easy. You can't just up and start running a marathon, Peyton."

"Yes, I know, but we're right in front of the restaurant and I have you by my side. Come on. I can do this," she said, looking at him with pleading eyes.

"Okay, I guess you do need to get used to putting weight on your ankles."

He ran around to her side and helped her out. With his arm on the small of her back, he carefully assisted her into the restaurant.

Much like they used to do in happier times, they laughed and talked when they were seated. Derek talked about the updates for a new App he had been working on. He said when he was done with it, he could stand to make even more millions than he did with the first App he designed during the beginning of their marriage.

"I'm so happy for you, Derek. I know it's going to be great. You're going to keep on until you're the next Steve Jobs or Bill Gates," she complimented.

Derek's smile broadened and an expression of satisfaction showed in his eyes. "Thanks, I'm going to claim that."

"Oh, did you know Harper started filming again for his TV show?"

"No, I didn't," Derek replied, pausing briefly when the server brought their food to the table. "I thought he was done with that. He hasn't had that show in at least five years, right?"

"Yeah, I know, but Eva said one of the television executives Harper operated on, was so thankful that Harper saved his life that he thought he should revitalize the show. So now it's going to be called *Matters of the Heart*. Eva filmed an episode with him too. Remember, I told you me and the girls were going to watch her. She prepared heart healthy meals that anyone can make at home."

"Yeah, but you didn't say it was for a show Harper was doing, but hey, that's cool. Seems like they're doing pretty good."

"Well, I guess you could say things are better. You know ever since she went back to him, they seem to be in a good space."

"They wouldn't be in a bad space if she hadn't cheated on the man, got pregnant, and then tried to tell him the baby was his." Derek shook his head in disgust.

"Yeah, I guess, but remember, she wasn't pregnant. She had some other issue. I can't think of the name of it," Peyton said, hating that she'd brought up Eva and Harper.

"Still, she was wrong, but if they can work through things, then good for them. To each his own." Derek put a forkful of food inside his mouth.

"Isn't it a beautiful day?" Peyton said, changing the subject. She didn't want to get into a debate about troubled marriages. It would be too easy to bring up their problems, and the day was going good so far. Peyton didn't want to do anything to ruin that. They were sitting outside on the restaurant's patio with an ocean view in the distance.

"Yeah, it is. Makes me dread going to the office."

"Then don't go," Peyton urged. "You hardly ever take off work, Derek. If you want to take the rest of the day, the week off even, then do it!"

"I would love to go surfing. I haven't done that in months," he said as he stared out at the horizon.

"I say call the office and let Matt know you're not coming in." Matt was the senior vice president. He was just as thorough as Derek so everything would be in good hands. Derek was an over achiever and could be somewhat of a workaholic. He rarely took time to relax and do some of the things he enjoyed, such as surfing. He was also a movie buff, but he rarely went to the movies like he used to do when they were first married. He either waited until they came out on DVD or television. Sometimes he would rent the movie from off the television, but even that was rare.

In addition to Matt, Derek had a great administrative assistant. She could handle just about anything Derek put in front of her. "You know Cheryl will let you know if anything urgent comes up. That woman can run that bank with her eyes closed. Besides, you act like you can't work from home. You have everything you need. Shucks, you can even work from your phone!" Peyton reminded him.

"You know what? You're right. I'm going to do it. Let's eat and when Liam gets home from school and lacrosse practice, we can ride to the beach. Liam could use some more surfing lessons," he said, smiling. "You'll have to sit on the sidelines and cheer us on," he joked and Peyton laughed.

She felt good. Maybe there was a chance for them after all. If she could keep her cool and stay away from the bottle, she might stand a chance at salvaging her marriage.

"You know you can't walk out on that sand, Peyton. I insist on you going in your manual wheelchair. Deal?"

"Deal," Peyton said, beaming as she stuck her fork in her Bolognese pasta.

Derek picked up his grilled chicken sandwich on a potato bun and took a big bite out of it with a huge grin on his face!

This is only the beginning, Peyton thought. *You're going to love me again.*

Chapter 15

"Letting go and forgetting the past is easier said than done, but never use the past as an excuse to not care about your future." Jayden Hayes

Meesha dashed out the door, got in her car, and headed to Perfecting Your Faith Academy. Since before she gave birth to now three-month-old Makena, she had spent very little if any time at the school that she loved dearly. For one, she was away from the Academy when she needed time away from Carlton. She and the boys went to Los Angeles to visit her sister, Geena. It was during all the mess going on with Breyonna, Liam, and the fact that Carlton wanted a divorce. The Academy was out for summer break during that time anyway, and she took the boys along. She needed to get away to gain some clarity of mind about what she needed to do concerning her marriage. If she was going to make a wise decision, she needed some time that she could set aside to pray and seek God for answers. God led her back to Adverse City and for now, she was glad she had listened and obeyed.

Since returning home, her marriage was thriving, the boys adored their baby sister, and Carlton's ministry was continuing to prosper. Everything was picture perfect, which meant she could go back to dedicating time to the Academy. The school was growing too, and there was an even longer waiting list for perspective students. The cap was 600 students because they wanted to maintain small classroom sizes with state of the art equipment, highly qualified teachers with Masters' degrees and above, and a curriculum that rivaled some of the best preparatory schools across the country.

She drove her luxury automobile into her reserved parking space. Meesha sat in the car for a while and watched as the students filed into the school. A smile complimented her flawless face along with a body that had returned to nearly perfect after having given birth to her fifth child.

People often remarked about her size and often asked how she maintained her perfect size four figure after having 'all those children'. The thing is, Meesha didn't have to work out much. She watched her diet, which consisted mostly of fruits, veggies, plenty of spring water, and what she often told the curious was she believed in having *lots of sex*. She and Carlton always enjoyed a healthy, active, fulfilling sex life. It suffered, of course, when they went through their marital turbulence, but even then, Carlton still desired her. Now all of that was behind them, and their sexual life was better than ever. Meesha had no complaints.

She refocused on the young people going inside the school. Some of the older kids drove their cars and Meesha watched as they parked in the Student Parking Only section of the school. Others were dropped off by parents. It was hustle and bustle. Grabbing hold of the door, she was about to get out of the car when she saw Avery drive up. She sat back against the seat and watched as Avery drove up close to the entrance of the school in the Student Drop Off area.

Meesha watched as Avery said something to the girls. Lexie, who was sitting in the front seat, leaned in and kissed her mother. Avery then leaned to the back while Heather leaned forward to the front and they hugged and kissed before both girls got out of the car and quickly began engaging with their friends.

Another couple, a teen couple, caught Meesha's eye and though she didn't want to, thoughts forced themselves into her mind about that awful period in her life. Tears immediately formed in her eyes as she watched the young couple walk hand in hand as they gazed lovingly at each other. She recognized them, had seen them time and time again at school and sometimes at church. If Meesha wasn't mistaken, the teens were in the Academy's senior class.

She quickly wiped away her tears. "Not today. Devil, you are a liar," she mouthed before getting out of the car. "I am forgiven. Forget those things that lie behind and forge toward those things that are ahead."

Sucking in her bout with anxiety over the thoughts of her sordid past, she opened the door, put one Louboutin cladded foot to the pavement, then the other, and boldly stepped out of the car. Her Brazilian weave swung with every step she made, and she carried her Gucci bag, a recent *just because gift* from Carlton, in her blinged out hand. Several parents and kids spoke to her as she walked toward the school entrance. Nothing was going to ruin her life. She had overcome, persevered, and prayed her way to where she was, and no devil in Hell was going to hold her back or cause her to stumble.

"Good morning, Mrs. Porter. It's good to have you back," the administrative assistant stated as soon as Meesha entered the school office. At the Academy most of the staff called her Mrs. Porter rather than First Lady Porter. She liked the fact that they distinguished the different roles of the two titles.

"Thank you and good morning to you too, Alice Faye. This is the day the Lord has made."

"Yes, it is, Mrs. Porter. We will rejoice and be glad in it," Alice Faye finished.

"Yes, praise the Lord, we will." Meesha waltzed past Alice Faye. Alice Faye watched Meesha's red bottoms grace the office floor like a gazelle.

Down the hall and into her office Meesha went. Once inside, she stopped, took a moment to peruse the space before she walked around to her desk, and set her keys and purse on the walnut and cherry desktop. She was where she belonged, and she couldn't be happier.

She got settled into the routine she had become accustomed to. There was always something that required her attention. She called Alice Faye into her office and assigned her the task of contacting several of their top donors to obtain their commitments for the upcoming school year. She also asked her to gather a list of perspective donors. They had a thriving Academy but it was only as good as their donors, and Meesha was glad she had some heavy hitters who didn't mind supporting the school with their money.

After Alice Faye left the office, moments later, there was a knock on her door at the same time her interoffice phone rang.

"Yes, Alice Faye?"

"Mr. Porter is on his way to your office. Kingston, that is," she clarified.

"Okay, that must be him knocking now. Thanks, Alice Faye." She pushed the Off button to the interoffice phone while simultaneously saying, "Come in."

In strolled Kingston Porter. "Welcome back, sis." He closed the office door behind him and approached her desk.

Meesha stood up and they embraced. "It's good to see you, Kingston," she said. "Yep, I'm back in the saddle," she said, and chuckled lightly.

Kingston wore many hats at Perfecting Your Faith. One was that of Assistant Headmaster of the Academy. Carlton's other brother, Martin, focused mainly on church administrative functions and staff.

"Are you ready for me to catch you up on what's been going on during your absence?"

"Yes, but first I want to get personal. We haven't talked much, but with a new baby in the house, among other things, I've been swamped. Tell me, how are you and Damica? Is the wedding still on?"

"Yes. She's doing all the planning, of course. She wants a fall wedding. That's fine by me. I just want to make her my wife," he said, beaming.

"Look at you, the man is in love," Meesha remarked and smiled. "I'm happy for you, Kingston. You're a good man and I know you're going to be a great husband and father to Damica's son."

"Yes, he's already like my son. I love that kid."

"Damica is blessed to have a man like you, but I think she knows that."

"I try to show her and J'elon every chance I get," Kingston replied. "I'm just as blessed to have found her. She's everything I've wanted in a woman, everything I prayed for."

"That's good, Kingston. Okay, enough of my probing. Let's get on with business."

"Whoa, hold up. I'm not going to let you off the hook that easy."

"What are you talking about?"

"What's going on between you and my brother? How is he treating you?"

"Things are good. I think we're finally in a good place again."

"Good. He better not mess up this go round. He has a good thing too you know. You're a good woman, Meesha, and a wonderful mother to my nephews, and to that beautiful little niece of mine."

"Thanks, Kingston. That means a lot coming from you. I know how much you admire your brother."

"As long as he does what's right, but I'm not going to be on his side when he's in the wrong. Remember, sis-in-law, I got your back. All you have to do is let me know if that chump gets outta line, and me and Martin will beat him up." Kingston leaned back in his chair and began laughing.

"Will do." Meesha laughed.

Chapter 16

"—I'm no cheek turner. . .You kill my dog, you better hide your cat." Muhammad Ali

"I'm leaving to go pick up the girls," Avery told RJ's nanny. Her girls loved attending the school that Meesha had partly been responsible for founding. The school had grown and was considered as one of the best private schools on Fisher Island and Miami Beach.

Unlike Meesha, Avery didn't have a permanent live-in nanny and housekeeper until RJ was born. Before giving birth to her son, she preferred to take care of her own children, relying on a babysitter only when she and Ryker had an outside engagement or entertained at home.

Avery soon accepted that Ryker had been right. The live-in nanny helped her a lot with not just RJ, but with Heather and Lexie, too. On occasion, Avery would spazz out—which is how she described it to her therapist— and refused to nurse her cute, chubby little boy. During her better days, she made sure she pumped and bottled as much of her breast milk as possible. She loved the little boy, but sometimes when she looked at him, all she could think about was the way Carlton had dismissed her and made light of what she thought they had together. Other days she was irritated or angry toward the girls and Ryker. The littlest things annoyed her, and there were times she felt resentment toward everyone in her inner circle. Feelings of sadness, emptiness, and numbness saturated her soul without giving her a moment's warning.

The weekly therapy sessions seemed to slowly help Avery, and she began to connect with the baby. She told Ryker that she was starting to feel better and insisted that he could let the nanny move out, but Ryker convinced her that the nanny should stay at least until RJ was six months old. After that, they could reevaluate the situation. Avery finally relented. She had to admit, if only to herself, that the nanny took a lot of pressure off of her and she was able to mentally take her time adjusting to raising an infant again. Heather and Lexie, now ages eleven and nine, could present a whole other set of pressure for the sensitive woman Avery was.

She left home early enough to make a pre-planned stop at one of the pharmacy stores she'd seen on her daily trek to take the girls to school. The plan she had devised would be put into motion as soon as she picked up the over the counter DNA test. Recently, she had received in the mail two Ancestry DNA kits she'd ordered. She easily convinced Ryker that it would be fun to find out about their family history.

After purchasing a DNA kit from the pharmacy, Avery chuckled as she drove to Perfecting Your Faith Academy. Avery's plan was to tell Ryker that he was taking the Ancestry DNA test, which he was, but what he wouldn't know and hopefully would never find out, was she was going to also do the over-the-counter test to determine if RJ was his kid. She wasn't going to be caught up like Peyton and Carlton were when it came to Liam's paternity. If RJ turned out not to be Ryker's son she would have her answer because that meant her baby's daddy was none other than the infamous, finer than Morris Chestnut, Pastor Carlton Porter.

"Ryker, the Ancestry DNA kit arrived today. Do you want to do it this evening? I got one for you and one for me," Avery told him later that evening.

Ryker was stretched out on the sofa in the family room watching an episode of "Power."

"Yeah, let's do it when this goes off. I want to see what Ghost is up to. I think Tommy is going to cross him," he said, referring to the characters on the popular cable network show.

"That's fine. I was just letting you know it came. I'm going to go upstairs and take my shower. When you're done watching that, just come on upstairs."

"RJ asleep?" he asked, looking over his shoulder at her.

"Yes, he might even stay asleep for most of the night. He's doing so much better sleeping longer."

"Yeah, he is."

"It's time we let him start sleeping in his crib, Ryker."

"We'll talk about it later. Whoa, I knew that was about to happen!" he said, when someone was shot on the show.

Avery threw up her hands, turned around, and walked out. There was no talking to Ryker when he was watching that show. Yet, she wasn't bothered by it at all—it was one of his few guilty pleasures. She was more concerned about him letting the nanny do her job and about RJ sleeping in his own room instead of between the two of them every night.

Tonight she had different plans. She had already talked to the nanny and told her that she wanted RJ to sleep in her room or she wanted the nanny to sleep in the room with RJ. Whichever one worked best for her, as long as Avery could have some alone-in-the-bed time with her husband.

The nanny more than agreed. She had talked to Ryker and Avery on more than one occasion about it being best for RJ to sleep in his own bed. It was safer that way and healthier. Now all Avery had to do was convince Ryker that RJ would be just fine sleeping with the nanny.

Ryker came upstairs an hour later. Avery had showered, gotten the DNA tests and the Ancestry DNA kits, together. After he took his shower, Avery approached him again about taking the test.

"Honey, are you ready to do the test?" she asked as he came out of the shower.

"Yeah, in a minute. Does the nanny have RJ?"

"Yes, and he's asleep. You remember what she told us, and how many times she's told us, Ryker. We have to let him sleep in his own crib."

"Too much can happen with him being in that room by himself. He can sleep in here. He has a crib in here. Plus, I don't see what's wrong with him sleeping in the bed with us until he's older."

"You know what she said. It's safer for him to be in his own bed, Ryker. We could easily turn over on him during the night and never know it. He can get underneath us and, well, I don't want to think about what could happen. Let's just try it for tonight. We can take one day at a time. She's going to sleep in his room with him, so we can see everything that's going on, on the monitor."

Ryker turned the monitor toward him, looked at it, and saw the nanny asleep on the twin bed they had in the room. RJ was sleeping soundly in his crib.

"We'll see how it goes," he said reluctantly.

Avery had already swabbed RJ's mouth and now she had to get Ryker still enough for him to take his test.

"You ready?"

"Yep, let's find out where we come from for real," he said, and laughed lightly.

Avery read the instructions out loud for the Ancestry DNA test. Ryker listened and when she was done she administered the test, only it was not for the Ancestry DNA; it was for the DNA test.

"That was painless," Ryker said.

"Oh, darn, I think I did it wrong."

"What do you mean you did it wrong?"

"I want you to do it again. I don't think you had enough saliva," she lied. "I'm glad I paid for an extra kit. Here you go. Do it again."

This time she used the Ancestry DNA test so she could have both tests taken.

"You bought three test kits?"

"Actually I bought four," she lied again. "I know how I can lose things so I thought better safe than sorry." She finished the test and returned the accessories to the container like the directions stated.

Ryker smiled at his wife, shook his head, and said, "You're so funny, Avery Mitchelson."

"That's why you love me," she replied.

He grabbed her by her butt and pulled her close to him while he sat on the bed.

"Let me go put this up so I can send it off first thing tomorrow. Then I'm all yours," she told him, kissing him on top of his head.

She turned around and he swatted her on the butt.

"Don't you start nothing you can't finish," she said, smiling.

"Oh, I plan to start and I plan to make it *wayyyy* past the finish line," he told her.

Her plan worked like a charm. She had both tests completed and ready to mail. She returned to the bed and for the first time in weeks, she slept like a baby, but only after she and Ryker made love like there would be no tomorrow.

Chapter 17

"Don't believe everything you hear: Real Eyes. Realize. Real Lies." Tupac Shakur.

As the days sailed by, Avery began feeling much better. Today was Sunday and she was up early to get herself and the baby ready for church and his christening ceremony. Meesha was having Makena's christening, too. It was the perfect plan coming together for Avery. When Meesha told her about the date of Makena's christening, Avery suggested that she have little RJ christened at the same time, to which Meesha readily agreed. She laughed at the thought of seeing Carlton squirm at having to dedicate a child to the Lord that could easily belong to him. *Stupid fool,* she thought.

Avery wondered how it would turn out. Would Carlton crumble when he held up RJ and presented the baby before God? She smiled a devilish smile.

"Heather…Lexie," she called, holding RJ and walking up the hall toward each of their bedrooms.

When she looked inside each of their rooms, she saw that the girls were practically dressed. Avery smiled. The girls were so beautiful. Since her struggle with postpartum depression they seemed to go out of their way to be extra quiet, be more mannerable, and bother Avery less than usual. Knowing Ryker as well as she did, Avery surmised that he had talked to them and that was the reason for their pleasant behavior and attitude toward her. She wasn't going to complain; she welcomed the bit of peace around an otherwise chaotic household with two little girls and a baby.

"Lexie, you look so pretty." Avery entered her room and took a seat in the corner chair. The dark pink dress with layered soft tulle was one of the new dresses Lexie had chosen on their recent shopping excursion with their daddy. The girls had him wrapped around their little fingers. There weren't too many times that he told them 'no.'

"Thank you, Mommy." Lexie twirled around and around before slipping her feet inside matching shoes.

Heather entered Lexie's room. "Mommy, I don't like my dress," she said with her lip downturned.

"Honey, you look beautiful. Didn't you pick out that dress when your father took you and Lexie shopping the other day?"

"Yes, but I don't like it."

Avery felt her mood shifting just that quickly. Heather could be a handful, especially when she didn't get her way. She had that same spitfire, turn on a dime, personality as Avery and it caused them to clash often.

"Look, it'll be fine. Lexie, tell your sister she looks pretty."

"I told you not to pick that one. Go put the other one on—the pink one," Lexie said instead.

"I don't want to wear the pink one. You have on pink." Heather began to pout and tear up.

RJ, as if sensing his sister's frustration, began to pout and let out a loud cry.

"See what you've done," Avery snapped. "Just go pick out another dress!"

"But...I—"

"I said, go pick out another dress or you're going to be sorry, Heather. I don't have time for your shenanigans this morning!"

RJ cried louder.

Avery stood up abruptly.

Thank God Ryker appeared. "Hey, what's going on?"

"I can't take it," Avery said. "You have them too spoiled. All I want to do is go to church and…" she pointed at Heather who was crying now and clinging to her father's pant leg. "You handle it." She pushed RJ into Ryker's arms and stormed out of Lexie's bedroom.

They know how to ruin my day," she mouthed as she went to her room and did the finishing touches on her makeup.

"Liam, sweetheart. You are such a handsome guy," Peyton complimented her son. "And you look dashing," she said, turning to Derek. "The two most handsome men in the entire world."

"And you look absolutely gorgeous this morning, doesn't she, son?"

"Yes, you look pretty, Mom."

Peyton had slimmed down considerably. Even when she was pounds heavier, she could dress and make herself look like a runway fashion model. Today was no different. Her teal and cream Yves Saint Laurent pantsuit showed her newly defined curves while the two mobilizers might have gone undetected if it wasn't for the slight change in her gait they caused and the bulky shoe portion of the brace.

At church, Meesha was seated in her usual space, on a row toward the front of the elegant sanctuary. The boys were in Children's Church and Makena was in the nursery, along with her nanny. She looked up and smiled broadly when she saw Peyton walking in on Derek's arm and Liam on her other side. Liam waited until Peyton sat down then turned and left out of the sanctuary and headed to Youth Church.

"It's good to see you walking. God is good."

"Yes, He is," Peyton said, smiled, and lightly tapped Meesha on the back of her hand. Derek leaned over and greeted Meesha with a light kiss on the cheek and a pat on her back.

Moments later, Eva and Harper and Avery and Ryker walked up. Eva and Harper joined Meesha, Peyton, and Derek on the same row while Avery and Ryker took seats on the row behind them.

Everyone greeted each other.

"Why don't you sit up here?" Peyton suggested.

Ryker showed his palm and shook his head. "No, we're good," he said with RJ in his arms.

"Did the girls go to Children's Church?" Eva asked.

"Yes, we dropped them off, thank God," Avery said, rolling her eyes upward. Ryker was not about to allow his son to go into the nursery. He had made it clear to Avery that RJ had to be basically walking and talking before he would leave his son. He did the same thing when the girls were small.

After making idle chatter for a few minutes, the ladies stopped whispering when the music started.

Carlton approached the podium after prayer and several songs from the choir.

Avery felt a lump form in her throat. Each time she laid eyes on Carlton, he looked finer than before, and this morning was no different. His black Armani suit and Ferragamo loafers matched his captivating swagger. It was enough to make her dizzy with lust as he stood in the pulpit.

Eva thought about the secret Avery had shared as she listened to Carlton's message about second chances.

"And the word of God says, then Jonah prayed to the Lord his God from the belly of the fish, saying, I called out to the Lord out of my distress and He answered me."

Carlton spoke freely, pulling from his vast memory of an abundant number of Bible passages. "Out of the belly of Sheol I cried, and you heard my voice. For you cast me into the deep, into the heart of the seas, and the flood surrounded me. All your waves and your billows passed over me. Perfecting

Your Faith, Jonah was disobedient. He refused to follow God's instructions. What happened to him because of his disobedience? You know the story."

Carlton looked around at his attentive congregation. He had them just where he wanted them, glued to his message and the words God had given him to speak. Each time he stood in the pulpit before his congregation, he was reassured that he was doing what he had been called to do as a youngster. He felt right preaching and teaching about God.

"Jonah landed in the belly of a whale," He continued as he began to slowly walk back and forth across the podium. "He was destined for death—destined for his life to end. But I'm here to remind somebody today that the God we serve is a God of second chances."

The congregation shouted praises and hallelujahs as Carlton delivered yet another powerful, soul-stirring, spirit-changing message.

"Has anybody here ever messed up? Have you messed up so badly that you just knew there was no way you would be forgiven, that you would ever recover? Did your friends, your family, and your loved ones turn their backs on you and kick you to the curb?"

People in the sanctuary began praising God, shouting, and the organist played musical scales that further ignited the on fire congregation.

"I'm standing before you today to say that we all have messed up at one time or another in our lives. But the good news is that we serve a God of second chances. I know I've told you this before, but my spirit says that somebody in here needs a reminder of the goodness of God. Just like God gave Jonah a second chance by rescuing him out of the belly of the fish, he will do the same for you." Carlton's voice boomed. "His mercies are new every morning."

Avery sat in her seat with a slight smile on her face. Arms

folded, and body rigid, she thought about the results of the DNA tests.

Carlton, like always, preached with fervor as he walked back and forth across the carpeted floors of the sanctuary.

At the end of his message, he invited people to come forward and they did. They came forth in droves—youth, young adults, middle aged, and seniors came. Carlton had that kind of drawing effect. They came to the front of the church to dedicate their lives to Christ, seek prayer, or join Perfecting Your Faith.

"Wow, your husband's sermons just get better and better," Harper said at the end of service. "The man is a dynamic speaker. God is using him."

Meesha blushed. "Yes, he is. Thank you, Harper."

Eva stood next to Harper, his arm securely around her waist where she couldn't ease out of his firm grasp even if she wanted to. Here they were, standing in front of Meesha like they were the perfect couple with the perfect marriage when things couldn't be farther from the truth. She stood next to Harper with a fake smile plastered across her face, but hurting and confused on the inside.

Harper continued talking. "I'm sorry that Eva and I couldn't accept the offer to be your little girl's godparents."

"No need for apologies. I understand that Avery and Ryker asked you first. It's not a problem, really. His brother, Martin and his wife, agreed to be her godparents. They're a wonderful couple."

"Yes, we know Brother and Sister Porter, and you're right, they are good people so that's good to know. For what it's worth, I've never told you that I appreciate you."

Meesha cut her eyes briefly at Eva. Eva rolled her eyes up in her head.

"Appreciate *me*. For what?"

"For being a good friend to my wife. I know you didn't agree with me when, well when she and I had our disagreement, but like Pastor Porter preached today, thank God we have a God who doles out second chances. I'm thankful I listened to him," he said and kissed Eva on top of her head.

"Yes, his message was quite timely. One thing about Carlton is he lets God use him and speak through him." *What in the world is wrong with Eva? She's acting like a zombie or something.*

"That he does," Harper said while Eva remained unusually quiet.

Meesha couldn't get over Eva's odd silence but thought it was not the proper time or place to address her concerns.

The nanny appeared with Makena and the boys and Avery walked up. Eva looked relieved.

"Would you like me to go get Heather and Lexie so they can be in here for the christening?" Eva turned and asked Avery.

"I can go get them," Avery answered.

"I don't mind. Really," Eva said. "After all, I *am* RJ's godmother. Let me do something to help." Eva smiled. "You and Ryker go on and get in place for the ceremony and I'll be right back."

"Okay, thank you, Eva." Avery smiled back.

Eva excused herself, pushed slightly against Harper's hold, and walked away. Everyone else made the short walk to the altar from where they were gathered.

Holding his sleeping son, Ryker appeared, turned, and then said to his wife, "You about ready?"

"Just as soon as Eva comes back with the girls, but we can go and get in position at the altar."

Avery looked around for Eva as she and Ryker made their way down to the altar. She saw Heather followed by Lexie and Eva. The three of them were laughing and chattering away. Avery wished that Eva would be able to one day have a child of her own, but she didn't think that would be possible as long as she remained with Harper. Harper didn't strike her as the type of guy who would get his vasectomy reversed or even adopt a kid. *Poor Eva.*

The christening ceremony was beautiful. Surprisingly, Carlton didn't seem to raise one iota of suspicion as he removed a still sleeping RJ from Ryker's arms, prayed over the baby boy, and then lifted him up toward the heavens as a symbol of returning him to God.

Carlton could only pray that the anxiety he felt when he picked up the little boy was not evident on his face or in his words. He looked at the sleeping baby, searching for any resemblance to himself. He saw none. He quickly looked at Avery whose gaze was fixed on him like concrete. It looked as if she had the slightest Mona Lisa like smile on her face. Was she gloating? *Demon,* he thought. *Wicked woman.*

He prayed over the little boy and then said a silent prayer to God that the child, like Liam, was not his. As long as Avery kept her crazy, delusional mouth shut, everything would be just fine. If she knew what was good for her, she wouldn't want to push him because he could be very unpleasant when he was pushed. So far, he had been able to keep her quiet, but the way she did little slick things from time to time to get under his skin was starting to aggravate him.

Eva and Harper stood on each side of Ryker and Avery. Eva watched the exchange between Avery and Carlton. The expression on his face showed guilt and worry. Maybe nobody else saw it, but she did, and glancing at Avery, she could tell that Avery sensed it too. *Good for him. He should be squirming,* Eva thought and flashed a smile his way.

He placed RJ back in Ryker's arms and moved on to his precious little girl and repeated the ceremonial blessing and christening over her life.

Meesha beamed with inexplicable joy as the godparents and her four boys stood before her husband and their father.

The couples, godparents, and their children went to lunch after the ceremony. The men talked mostly sports and work while the housewives discussed family, children, Eva's love of culinary school, Peyton's positive recovery, and other small talk.

The children, minus Liam, were somewhat mischievous, but that was normal. Liam kept his head glued to his phone, seemingly oblivious to everything going on around him.

By the time the final course of their meal arrived and they indulged in the scrumptious food, the afternoon was drawing late and the babies were starting to get cranky. Meesha's nanny tended to Makena when she began to fuss. RJ followed with a bellow of his own. Ryker comforted the little boy by removing him from his stroller and cradling him in his arms. He pulled out a bottle of fresh pumped breast milk from the portable cooler. He asked the server to warm it. When the server returned with the warm bottle of milk, Ryker fed his son.

Avery felt herself becoming moody and suddenly demanded that they leave the restaurant.

Ryker didn't put up a fuss. He gathered the girls, the baby… and his wife. They said their goodbyes and were the first couple to depart.

Chapter 18

"Secrets are lies by another name." Michael Murpugo

Peyton spent hours online and, on the phone, talking to Adverse City's most sought after party planner. Derek's thirty-ninth birthday was in a few weeks. It may not have been a milestone birthday, but it was his birthday nonetheless, and she was going to make sure it was the best birthday bash in Adverse City.

Entertaining had never been quite her forte, but when she did entertain she pulled out all stops. Because Derek was more of a reserved type of man with a select number of what he considered *true friends*, she limited the 'invitation only' list to one hundred people consisting of family, friends, coworkers and a select number of his biggest bank customers.

"I will have everything just as you requested," Lawrence Jakobe, the million dollar party planner assured her on video chat. "The invitations have gone out. You've tasted the cake and chosen it. You have all the decorations selected, and the color scheme is going to be perfect. Outside on the back lawn will be a huge decorated party tent. All you need to do now is finalize the food. You haven't changed your mind about a sit down dinner have you? I know you were thinking of a buffet too," Lawrence went on and on.

"I think it would be more sophisticated and more to Derek's liking if we have a sit down dinner. However, I still want h'ordeuvres, finger foods, and a variety of desserts and beverages, but please, remember there is to be no liquor of any kind."

"Are you sure? What's a party without at least a little alcohol?" Lawrence said, raising a questioning eyebrow.

"A safe party and a fun party. I'm sure you can make it work. You can have all sorts of virgin drinks."

"Oh, certainly. Do not worry. I'm on it," Lawrence agreed.

"As you should. I'm paying you enough," Peyton barked slightly, but reined her rising attitude back in. She had been doing most, if not all, of the planning while Derek was at the office since it was going to be a surprise. Liam was in on it and helped to keep his dad occupied on the occasions when Derek was at home and Peyton needed to handle something concerning the party.

The doorbell rang. "Okay, Lawrence, I promise to finalize the food choices later this evening or first thing tomorrow."

"Yes, Mrs. Hudson. That will be fine."

"Great. Well someone is at the door. We'll chat later."

"Yes, of course," Lawrence replied and they disconnected from video chat.

Peyton's personal assistant knocked on the door of the study. "Come in."

"Mrs. Hudson, Mrs. Stenberg is here."

"Oh, great. Please show her in."

"Of course." The assistant disappeared and returned with Eva.

"Please bring the other ladies in here too when they arrive," Peyton told the personal assistant.

"Yes, I sure will," the assistant responded.

"Hey, girl. How are things going?"

"Good, I guess, considering the party is in a few weeks and I still have a ton of things I need to finish."

"Everything is going to turn out just fine. Avery and Meesha should be here in a few minutes. We're all going to sit down and together we'll make sure everything is the way you want it to be. Derek is going to be so surprised and happy."

"I sure hope so, Eva."

The doorbell rang again and this time Meesha was led into the study.

"Hi, ladies," Meesha said as she entered the room.

"Hi, Meesha," Peyton and Eva said.

Eva's text notifier chimed. She looked at the phone in her hand and read the message.

```
Sorry, I don't feel up to coming. Need
some me time. You girls go on without me.
```

"Avery just texted me. She's not coming. Says she doesn't feel up to it."

"She's still battling with PPD, huh?" Peyton acknowledged.

"Yes, she is. Some days are better than others for her," Eva stated.

"I'm blessed and thankful that I didn't go through it as tough as she's experiencing. I mean I got the blues for a few days with the boys, but nothing like what poor Avery is experiencing," Meesha said.

"Well, I don't know a thing about it," said Peyton. "And from the sound of it, I don't want to ever know about it."

"Neither do I," Eva added.

"If you were just talking about depression, which I've heard PPD has similar symptoms, then I can identify with that," Peyton chimed in.

"Yeah, it *is* similar," Meesha agreed. "We have to continue to pray for her and be there for her as her friends."

"Right, and she'll be fine. She's still seeing a therapist. I think because of that she's getting better every day," Eva said.

"I'd hate for her to try to kill herself like she tried before," said Peyton.

"Peyton?" Meesha said.

"Well, I'm just saying. I hope she doesn't try to take herself out. It would be a shame to leave those children motherless."

"Let's change the subject," Eva said.

Meesha clapped her hands, laughed, and said, "Yes, you're right. Enough of this Debbie Downer talk. Let's get this show on the road. We have the best birthday party ever to pull off for your man."

"Oh yeah, you got that right," Peyton agreed and laughed and so did Eva.

"I still want to prepare a dish, something delectable, for the party," Eva told Peyton.

"I appreciate the offer, but this is going to be a one hundred percent catered affair, and I already have the caterer. When you get your own restaurant, you already know you'll have my business. Your food is delicious, at least the one dish I've tasted." Peyton laughed.

"Don't play," Eva said and chuckled.

"Seriously, you *can* cook."

"Thanks, Peyton. That's the first time I've heard you give a compliment."

Eva and Meesha laughed again.

"Don't you all start," Peyton said and laughed with them. "Okay, come over here. What I need from you ladies is help deciding on the food. Let me pull up the sample menus."

At home, Avery hid away in her bedroom. She didn't have to pick up the girls today. They had dance class after school, and Ryker offered to pick them up, which was fine by her. The nanny was tending to RJ.

Avery curled up in her bed where she'd been ever since the girls and Ryker left earlier that morning. At first, her intention was to go over to Peyton's and help with the planning of Derek's surprise birthday party but the more she thought about it, the less she wanted to go. She didn't want to look into Meesha's face and pretend that all was fine when she couldn't stand Meesha right now.

Today was also the day she was supposed to be able to go online and view the results of the DNA test by using the preassigned password she received when she purchased the kit.

She channel surfed and stopped when she saw an episode of Paternity Court. Her eyes and ears became glued to the show. What was she going to do if RJ was Carlton's kid? Better yet, what would Carlton do? Surely, he would leave Meesha then— he had to. Her mind felt all jumbled and confused. She really didn't want to leave Ryker and chance losing her girls. What was she thinking? She shook her head from side to side as if she could shake some sense into her thoughts. She wanted to tell her therapist about what she was going through but she didn't feel she could trust her like that. Not with a secret like this.

She stopped when she saw the woman on the TV screen start crying when the judge told her that the man she had accused was not her twins' father. Avery watched the show often. She'd seen similar outcomes over and over again. How this show, like Maury, could still be on the air was a mystery, but she guessed it was people like her who fed its ratings.

On the bed next to her, Avery reached for her MacBook. She was nervous but she was ready to find out who RJ belonged to. She pushed the Power button on the laptop and while waiting on the screen to light up, she whispered a prayer. "God, if this baby is Carlton's let him do right by me and by his son. If the DNA results show that RJ belongs to Ryker, help me to accept it and move on with my life. Amen."

She went to the site, accessed the results, and read them carefully. When she read the results just like the woman on Paternity Court, Avery began sobbing and pounding the bed with her fists repeatedly. She could hear in her mind the judge telling her, "This man is not your baby's father."

"You have to be the father, Carlton. This can't be right. This cannot be," she screamed and cried. She and Ryker hadn't had sex during that time. Had they? Obviously they had because the tests showed that Ryker was RJ's daddy.

Avery cried on and off for hours. She finally stopped long enough to close down the DNA site before she powered off her Macbook. She curled up in a fetal position and remained in bed the rest of the day feeling sullen and lost.

When the nanny brought RJ in for his three o'clock feeding, she told her to get some of the stored breast milk to feed the crying baby. She didn't want to be bothered, and the last thing she wanted to do was nurse. Not now. Her mind was still playing weird tricks on her and she needed time to soak in what the test revealed.

Somehow she had to move on with her life, just like she told God she would do. Now that she knew the truth, she would tell Carlton, or would she? Maybe she would let him remain in the dark. It would serve him right if she did. *Yes, I think I just might let you stew in your own pot of soup for a while, Carlton Porter. It'll serve you right for all you put me through.*

Chapter 19

"Sometimes the best things in life are the things you never see coming." Buffy Andrews

Peyton reserved a small private parking garage for all the guests with a limo service to transport them to her and Derek's ten thousand square foot mansion.

Meesha, Carlton, Avery, and Ryker looked like they were ready for TMZ to show up at any minute. Eva looked stunning, minus Harper who was called to the hospital earlier that afternoon. Eva hadn't heard from him since, and frankly couldn't be happier that she was solo. She wanted to enjoy herself and she couldn't do that with Harper. She didn't know what would set him off. Lately, things had been civil between them. He hadn't had any more of his abusive flare-ups, and Eva slowly, but still on pins and needles, began to relax a bit. When he told her he was called to the hospital, she breathed a welcomed sigh. *Thank God for small miracles*, she thought as she walked into Peyton and Derek's lavish home.

As Eva mingled with her friends outside under the lanai, feet away from the party tent awaiting the guest of honor's arrival, she was quite surprised to see the handsome stranger from the rescue shelter as one of the guests. She watched him closely without him noticing. He was standing with a much older, attractive, silver-haired woman. The woman looked absolutely radiant and sophisticated, and Eva could tell that she was worth millions when she saw the sparkling diamonds dripping from around her neck, ears, and hands. She reeked of high society and money—lots of it.

Avery stood next to Eva and spoke lightly into her ear as she watched Eva staring in the lady's direction. "That's Meredith Winters. Can you believe she's eighty-seven years old? She can pass for at least sixty any day. She's been well preserved. Plastic surgery does do wonders. From what Ryker says, she adores Derek. She's his best customer. Has her millions in his bank, at least as much as his bank can handle. I'm sure the amount of wealth she has is spread over numerous investments and banks. She is after all, Adverse City's wealthiest woman. Our money is pennies compared to what that old lady has."

"Yes, I've heard of her, but I've never met her or seen her in person."

"She doesn't run in our circles, girl."

"I bet she doesn't. Who are those two men with her?"

"Her grandsons. The one on her right was recently married. That's his wife standing next to him. I can't believe you didn't read about it. He had a wedding that would rival the royal couple. Peyton and Derek went to it, of course."

"Oh, yeah, I remember when Peyton told us about that wedding. And the one on the left? Who is he?"

"You mean that fine specimen of a man?" Avery remarked and smiled with lust.

"Yes, fine he is…." Eva smiled and looked at Avery.

"That's her other grandson. His name is Quentin. He's someone you definitely should get to know."

With flinched eyebrows and a pull back of her neck, Eva looked at her best friend. "Why would I want to meet him? I mean he is definitely fine but I'm a married woman."

"Girl, please. I said that because you want to be a chef and own your own restaurants, right?"

"Yes, but what does that have to do with him?"

"He has a thriving restaurant in France, another one in New York, and not to mention a boatload of money himself, thanks to grandmommy dearest and to his own good fortune. In addition to him being a five-star chef, he and his brother are real estate tycoons. According to Ryker, Quentin recently moved back to Adverse City to help take care of his aging grandmother. She's the one that raised him and his brother after their parents died in a terrorist attack overseas where they lived when they were kids."

That may explain his accent, Eva thought as she listened to Avery.

"Quentin returned to Paris after he graduated from Wharton School of Business. That's where he opened the restaurant. It's at the top of the restaurant and food chain over there from what I've heard. So is the one in New York. He's also some kind of an animal enthusiast."

"Who would have guessed?"

"What did you say?" Avery asked.

"Oh, I was just saying, maybe you're right. Maybe he *is* someone I should meet."

"I thought that little resume' of his might make you change your mind."

"No, it's not the money, if that's what you mean, but I can't lie, it doesn't hurt the situation." Eva smiled slightly, not telling Avery that she had already met the handsome Quentin Winters.

"I bet. I'll see if I can get Ryker to introduce you sometime tonight. He handles Mrs. Winters and her grandsons' legal matters."

"Okay, that might work, but don't force it," Eva stated and they both started talking about something else.

"Don't you agree that Peyton should be proud of herself? I

mean, this party is it, girl. The grounds look amazing and the menu, decorations, everything is better than I could ever have pictured. You know, this might be the icing on the cake that will get her and Derek back together."

"Avery, I think you might be right," Meesha intervened as she appeared from out of nowhere and stood next to Eva without Avery seeing her come up. "I sure hope so."

"Yeah, me too," said Eva.

"How are you tonight, Miss Lady?" Eva asked Meesha.

"Fabulous. It's good to get out. Carlton and I have been cooped up in the house all week long. Other than me going to the Academy and him going to the church office, it's been uneventful. And with the kids, we hardly have much time to be alone. This is a welcome relief. It's actually our first date night again since Makena was born. It feels amazing."

"Good for you," Avery mumbled.

"What did you say?" Meesha asked.

"I said, good for you…and Carlton."

"You good?" asked Ryker as he walked up next to Avery and spoke into her ear.

"Yes, I'm fine. Thanks for being concerned," she turned to face him and said so that Meesha, in particular, couldn't hear, "but I'm not a china doll. I'm not going to break, Ryker. I'm feeling better this evening than I've felt in a long time."

He kissed her on the cheek. "You're *my* china doll, and I'm glad to hear that you're feeling good tonight. I want you to have fun."

"Don't worry, I'm not going to do anything to embarrass you," she said and grabbed hold of his hand as she caught Carlton looking at her with suspicion from a distance.

Avery returned Carlton's glare with a wicked smile of her own as if warning him not to cross her. She continued to toy with the findings of the DNA results and still played with the idea about whether she should go on and let Carlton off the hook and tell him about it. Then again she reason, RJ wasn't his kid so she didn't owe him an explanation about anything. She would leave things as they were for now and enjoy the evening. She didn't want to do or say anything that would mess things up for Peyton.

The guests continued to mix and mingle until Meesha and the ladies received a text from Peyton telling them they were on their way with Derek.

Peyton's plans couldn't have worked out any better. This evening's weather was perfect. She, Derek, and Liam had attended Liam's lacrosse game. After a big win by his team, they stopped at a deli to have a quick sandwich, and to talk about the game. Derek suggested they get something heavier to eat, but Liam told his parents that he had plans to go hang out with some of his teammates after he got home and changed. Derek agreed that in that case they should go home.

The plan was for Liam to leave home for the evening after they said, 'Surprise' to his dad. Unbeknownst to Derek, Liam and Peyton had already made plans for the teen to spend the night at his best friend's house after they went and celebrated his team's win.

Derek's birthday wasn't until the following Monday so he shouldn't have suspected a thing, especially a birthday party.

Peyton smiled as they entered the house, walked inside, and all was dark. The lights automatically came on in the smart home as they entered. There were no telltale signs of anything out of the ordinary going on, and Peyton released a satisfying smile as she walked between Derek and Liam.

As they made their way deeper inside the expansive residence, Peyton slightly eyed Liam and smiled.

"Something's going on," Derek said and halted his step.

"What do you mean? What is it?" Peyton asked.

"You guys hold up right here. Let me check this out."

"Check what out?" Peyton asked, feigning concern, but smiling inside as she saw the plan unfolding perfectly.

"Look, see the stream of flight coming in through the family room from outside. That shouldn't be. Looks like the sliding door leading to the back yard is open. Stay right here," he said again, holding his hand back, cautioning them not to move.

"Be careful, Derek," Peyton said, with a fake nervousness in her tone.

Derek walked farther into the family room and took cautious steps toward the sliding doors. He reached out, pushed one of the doors back, and it disappeared inside the wall.

Peyton and Liam walked up behind him. Derek looked absolutely stunned when an array of lights came on like bursts of sunlight shining through the dark.

"Surprise!" the guests said in perfect unison. Cell phone cameras flashed, videos started being recorded, and the hired photographer and videographer took picture after picture.

Derek stood like a mannequin for a moment, taking in the display of people standing before him. Next, he looked over at Liam then to the other side at Peyton. He released a big grin that filled his face with pride.

Peyton hugged him and Liam embraced his dad as people clapped.

Derek walked further into the open outside space and his eyes continued to brighten at the sight of his friends. He saw the lavish setup and it looked like tears sparkled in his eyes under a perfect moonlit night. He may not have been the kind of man who liked surprises, but this was a welcomed one. It was an evening he would surely remember for a long time to come—so would Peyton.

Chapter 20

"Until the lion learns to write, every story will glorify the hunter." African Proverb

The band jammed the latest tunes and the lead singer was amazing. Eva, Avery, and Meesha gossiped and did the fashion police thing about all the guests until Ryker came up, took her by the hand, and whisked Avery to the dance floor. She looked over her shoulder at Eva and Meesha with a smile on her face, shrugging her shoulders happily.

Carlton walked up seconds later and practically did the same to Meesha. Eva was left standing alone with a half-smile plastered on her pretty face. She decided to go to the casita that Peyton had set up for her guests. It had two bathrooms a small living space, and a bedroom.

The way Peyton had the casita arranged for the evening made it the perfect space for the female guests to refresh themselves, use the bathroom, and chill for a minute rather than having to go all the way back inside the main house. She had done the same thing for the men by rearranging the pool house as a space for them, which was a neat idea.

Following the decorated, paved walkway leading to the casita, she eyed the exquisite decorations and marveled at the extent and expense Peyton had gone through to make this evening special and perfect for Derek.

Eva entered the casita, went inside the restroom, relieved herself, and then went to the vanity to wash her hands and refresh her light makeup.

Exiting the casita, she headed back up the lit walkway toward the party tent.

"So, we meet again," the magnetic voice said, causing Eva to once again stumble. She didn't have to look around to know that it was *him*. She felt his arm steady her and she gazed up and into his deep sandy brown eyes. The scent of his cologne, mingled with the gentle breeze of the evening, could easily have taken her breath away, but she placed one hand over her chest as if to calm her rapidly beating heart. Why did this man have this type of effect on her?

"I guess we do," Eva replied like a bashful schoolgirl.

He flashed a warming smile at her. "So you know these folks, huh?"

"Yes. Peyton is a close friend. And you?"

"Yes, Derek has been my grandmother's financial advisor and banker for quite some time. She adores the guy."

"Quentin…Quentin Winters," he said, as he stopped walking and extended his hand toward Eva.

"Eva Stenberg," she responded, placing her hand inside his.

"Nice to finally officially meet you," he said and they continued their walk toward the party tent. "This is a cool party. Looks like his wife went all out for this affair."

Eva nodded in agreement. "Yes, everything is perfect."

They arrived at the tent and Eva almost immediately spotted Avery, who gave her a smile and a quick nod as Ryker clung to her like they were fresh newlyweds.

Eva scanned around the space further, and saw Peyton mingling with the guests. Meesha and Carlton were in a circle engaged in conversation with several other couples, and Derek, like his wife, was engaging with the guests. Peyton was the perfect hostess. Whether she thought so or not, she was in her element. She looked happier than she had in a long time, and Eva was happy for her.

When it was time for the five-course dinner to be served, Peyton was escorted to the front of the tent by the party planner. "May I have your attention please," Peyton said as she stepped up to where the band was located and spoke into the microphone. "We're going to enjoy another performance by the band. When they're done please go to your assigned tables and be seated so you can be served."

The band played a familiar, slow tune.

"May I?"

"May you what?" Eva responded.

"Have this dance?"

Eva raised her hands and shook her head. "Uh, no, I...I'm not the world's best dancer. You should know that after I've stumbled the three times we've ran into each other."

Quentin chuckled. "You mean twice," he playfully corrected, as he gently placed his hand at the small of her back.

Actually, it has been three times. I first saw you at Central Park about a year ago, she started to say but decided against it. Instead she said, "I don't know what it is but it seems that when—"

"When you're around me, you get all weak in the knees." He flashed another charming smile her way.

"No...that is not what I meant," she said quickly.

Quentin stood in front of her, and looked at her like he was seeing her for the first time. He studied her features, looked at the outline of her face. He thought back to when he saw her across the street from his pet store. When he stood at her car that day, he felt their paths had crossed before, but he couldn't remember where. He'd seen his share of beautiful women, but this one was different. There was a certain something about her that captivated him and he wanted to learn more about her.

"No need to take offense. I was just kidding, but you're right. I guess I stand corrected about the number of times you've almost fallen around me. The good thing about it is you know what they say about the number three, right?" He grabbed hold of her hand.

"No, actually I don't. What do they say?"

"It means you can't say no to dancing with me." He led her to the dance floor and pulled her gingerly into his arms as the slow jam played.

The band was on point. The lead singer of the group, a Lauren Hill lookalike, song the melodic, love song, *The First Time Ever I Saw Your Face* by Roberta Flack.

Without intentionally doing so, and more out of relaxing and listening to the words of the song, Eva rested her head against Quentin's broad chest as the space closed between them. Her arms felt secure and safe around his neck, and his hands around her torso made her feel some type of way.

She didn't see Harper when he appeared and stood outside the tent watching like a lurking voyeur. All she cared about at this moment *was* this moment. Eyes closed, she listened to the words of the song. It described exactly how she felt. *"I felt all flushed with fever, embarrassed by the crowd..."*

Harper watched and anger filled his eyes. He had made a horrible mistake marrying a girl like Eva. She was ten years his junior and she was nothing more than the equivalent of poor white trash. He had pulled her out of the gutter from where she came, what had he been thinking. He thought he was being led by God when he met her in Bolivia during his mission trip, but boy had he been wrong. Instead of the perfect wife, he had brought home a cheating, unappreciative, little slut who repaid him by sleeping with his son, and not the beautiful, sweet, innocent young woman who was the woman he'd prayed for God to send him.

Look at her. Guess she's found her next unsuspecting victim. His jawline twitched and a look of disbelief, rage, and frustration shrouded his face. Eyes hooded, mouth pursed, he looked like an evil villain. *An eye for an eye will never be enough.*

Harper walked up to Eva and Quentin, took her by her elbow, and gently pulled her out of Quentin's hold.

"Excuse me, Quentin. If you don't mind, I'd like to dance with my wife," he said with a broad smile plastered on his handsome face.

Eva was stunned to see him as she stepped back. She was also quite surprised to hear Harper call Quentin by his name. The two of them knew each other? Was this a setup of some sort to see how she would react to him and then he would run back and tell Harper a bunch of lies?

Quentin nodded and said, "Of course." He gave Harper dap. "I…uh…didn't know this was your wife," Quentin apologized, as if he had some reason to. "I heard you got married a while back. You finally tricked someone into marrying you." Quentin and Harper laughed.

Harper said, "You mean you didn't tell this guy you were married?" he looked at Eva quizzically.

"I…"

Quentin quickly spoke up, "It's the first thing she told me when I asked her to dance. She just didn't tell me she was married to *you*, bruh, and I don't blame her. I wouldn't tell anyone I was married to you either," Quentin joked and the men laughed again as Harper pulled Eva in close to him.

"Well, thanks for the dance," Quentin said, smiled and turned to walk off.

"Hold up, Quentin," Harper said as the song ended and the band began playing an upbeat tune.

Quentin turned back around and looked at Harper and at Eva. She looked like a frightened kitten.

"You look confused, my darling," Harper said, looking

down at his wife. "Let me explain. Quentin's grandmother is Emma Winters. She and I are longtime friends. She is one of Adverse General Hospital's biggest donors. She funded the Winters Cardiology Trauma Center which was a multimillion-dollar addition to Adverse General. She's also a well-known philanthropist known throughout Adverse City and Miami. And this guy here," Harper said, pointing to Quentin while the music stopped and people began filing to their assigned seats, "is a renowned chef and an animal activist. I don't know exactly how he mixes the two but, hey, it is what it is. I guess you could say he's one of the good guys, but I wouldn't tell him that," Harper teased.

"It's nice to officially meet you, Quentin, and learn so much about you and your grandmother. Harper, I'm so glad you were able to get away from the hospital and come to the party. If you'll excuse us…Quentin, we should go find our seats," she said as she grabbed Harper's hand.

"Well, the lady speaks and I listen," Harper said to Quentin. "Let's talk soon. We haven't had a chance to catch up since I heard you moved back to Adverse City."

"Sure thing," Quentin replied. "And thank you, Mrs. Harper for the pleasure of dancing with me." He smiled and did a half bow before he turned and walked away.

"You arrived just in time for dinner," Eva remarked as they walked toward the tables with silver nameplates of each guest engraved in deep bold black letters. They found their names and sat at their assigned table, which was the same table that Avery, Ryker, Meesha, and Carlton were seated. Derek and Peyton were seated at a head table along with Emma Winters, her grandsons, and Derek's brother and grandfather, who were well-respected investment bankers and financial wizards residing in Jacksonville. Peyton's parents did not attend for whatever reason, but Derek didn't seem to mind. He looked like he was having the best time of his life.

It was almost two thirty in the morning when the party came to an end. "Did the limo service bring you?" Eva asked Harper.

"No, I didn't park in the designated garage. Since I knew the party was well underway, I drove directly here and parked on the grounds. You can ride home with me. We'll pick up your car from the garage tomorrow after church."

"Okay," Eva agreed. "She would have rather taken the ride back to the garage with the limo service and drive her own car home, but now was not the time to ruffle Harper's feathers. He could wear the perfect mask for others but she never knew what real colors were laying underneath his public persona. She could tell from the tug on her elbow when she was dancing with Quentin that he was perturbed, but again he put on a real first class act in front of him. She prayed that tonight he would be kind, sweet Harper, and not the monster she had discovered he could swiftly turn into.

The drive home started off with the both of them being quiet. It was minutes before three o'clock in the morning, so there wasn't much to say. They were both exhausted. "It was a nice party," Harper said, breaking the thick, uneasy wall of silence between them.

"Yes, I think Derek really enjoyed himself. He and Peyton were all over the place, dancing, laughing, mingling, and having fun. I can't believe she was able to dance like that with those things on her legs." Eva chuckled.

"Yeah, she was getting her dance on for sure," Harper said and smiled as he stopped for the red traffic light. "And the food was perfect. Maybe you'll be able to have your own catering company one day. You *are* still enjoying your culinary classes, right?"

"Yes, I love school. I'm learning so much. We've started preparing a variety of meat dishes. It's so much fun. I can't wait until I can have my own restaurant."

"You haven't mentioned having your own restaurant before," Harper replied and looked at Eva before driving off after the light turned green.

He was right; she hadn't said anything to him about opening up a restaurant and that was her intention since this monster side of him had revealed itself. She didn't want him to know any of her future plans, but she had said it before she knew it. "Yeah, it's just something I've thought about after one of our instructors brought it up. She was telling us some of the avenues we could take as a chef."

"As long as you have the proper financing, I'm sure you could do it. But I know you, Eva, I'm sure you're going to make sure you have the money you need."

"What does that mean?" Eva asked, looking at him and hoping this wasn't going to lead to where she thought it might.

"Did you know Quentin Winters is a five-star chef? He owns several highly successful restaurants both in Paris and in New York?"

"No, really? Then again, how would I know any of that? I mean, I barely know the man's name. We had one dance, Harper. We didn't discuss our life history. I didn't know you were friends with Emma Winters. I've heard you mention her name a time or two, but I didn't know you had a relationship with her."

"Yes, Lady Winters, that's what I call her, and I are very good friends. I am also her cardiologist. I don't have a private practice anymore because of my other responsibilities, but who will turn away Emma Winters? The woman has done so much for my medical career and for Adverse General. Heck, she's done a lot for Adverse City period. I performed open-heart surgery on her, saving her life about twenty years ago. She's never forgotten it."

"I'm sure she hasn't. You're a great doctor, Harper."

"Thank you, sweetheart." Harper looked at Eva again, reached over and kneaded her hand with his, and smiled before refocusing his attention back on the road. The car became silent once again and Eva relaxed her head against the seat of the car, closed her eyes, and drifted off into a light sleep.

She woke up as they entered their community and Harper turned onto their street. He drove into their driveway, pushed the remote above his head to open the garage, and steered his black on black Range Rover inside.

Turning off the vehicle, he looked over at Eva.

"What?" she said.

"Oh, nothing. I was thinking about the first time I saw you. You were beautiful. So innocent looking. I think I fell in love with you instantly," he said.

Eva smiled but inside she was cautious, wondering where this was leading.

Harper opened his door and hurried around to Eva's side, and opened the door wider just as she opened it for herself.

"Tell me something, sweetheart."

Eva stepped down out of the car. "Yes, what is it?"

"How long have you been doing Quentin Winters?"

Chapter 21

"To be wronged is nothing…unless you continue to remember it." Confucius

"Thank you, Babe."

He did it again—called me Babe. "Did you have a good time? Were you really surprised?"

"Did I have a good time? Do you even have to ask? It was the best party I've ever been to, even though it was mine." He chuckled as he removed his clothes and hung each item in its proper place inside the closet. He was a stickler for organization, but so was Peyton—when she wasn't drinking. Those items that needed to be washed he opened the small door inside his very own humungous walk-in closet and dropped them down a built-in laundry chute.

Peyton stood inside the door of the closet, watching his every move, as they engaged in pleasant conversation like they were the happiest married couple on earth.

She laughed along with him. "I'm glad you had a good time. It seems like everyone enjoyed themselves."

"And you asked if I was surprised, yes, I had no idea. I mean, you know I usually don't like surprises, but this was an exception. The people were the ones I would have invited had

I planned it myself. I don't know if there were any you invited that didn't come, but it was just the right amount of people and everything was absolutely perfect. The food, the band, and seeing my brother and grandfather was the icing on the cake. Oh, and Miss Emma came, too. That was special. When I walked into the house and I saw that light from the family room, I was thinking someone broke into our house. But then, I said to myself that was highly unlikely with all the security systems we have installed. I would have received a notification of the house being breached or something. I didn't know what to think. Then when I went to check things out, pulled the door back, seeing and hearing everyone screaming *surprise*…man, it took a minute for me to digest what was going on. It was crazy."

Derek was down to his boxer briefs. Peyton looked at him hungrily.

"Aren't you going to get undressed?" he asked and walked out of his closet.

"Yes." She backed away and slowly walked towards her own closet on the other side of their bedroom. She had become accustomed to walking in her mobilizers, but she looked forward to next week when the doctor would give the okay for her to wear regular shoes again.

"Do you need my help?"

"No, I'll be fine."

"I'm going to take a shower then."

"Sure you don't want to wait on me?" she casually teased, not expecting him to agree.

"Yeah, I'll wait."

Peyton stopped dead in her tracks when he agreed, but said nothing. Everything had been perfect up until now and she did not want to do or say anything that might ruin that.

Undressed down to her red bikini bottoms, she picked out a sexy piece of lingerie. With gown in hands, she stepped out of her walk-in closet with her perky full mounds in full view of her husband. From the look she saw on Derek's face, he was quite pleased with what he witnessed.

Before losing close to twenty pounds, she was considered thick. She would never be a size two, four, or even a size eight like the other ladies, but she was still pleased with her body. Even as a full figured girl, Derek never once complained.

Dang, she looks sexy as all get out. Derek's thoughts and his manhood betrayed him. Even if he wanted to, and he didn't, he couldn't deny his desire for his wife. Since she had stopped drinking, he entertained the thought of staying in the marriage. The only thing was he still had doubts and trust issues when it came to Peyton. As much as he wanted to believe that drinking was a part of her past, the other part of him was still leery. He couldn't deal with it if she returned to the bottle.

If you're going to pray don't worry if you're going to worry, don't pray, the voice in his head reminded him. He had done his share of praying for his marriage, for the whole thing with Liam, for his wife's drinking, and so much more. God had come through every time in one way or the other. It wasn't always as he hoped but he could always rest assured it was for his good. This was no different. He couldn't worry about what tomorrow might bring. It was time to thank God for the changes Peyton had already made and forget those things that were in the past. He reached for his wife's hand, and led her into their bathroom.

"I had a good time at the party, did you?" Meesha asked as she and Carlton lay in their bed.

"Yes, Peyton really outdid things. If she called herself pulling out all the stops to save her marriage, then I'd say tonight was a big plus for her. It was grand."

"Yeah, it was. Derek couldn't have looked happier. I've been praying for their marriage and for God to completely deliver Peyton from drinking."

Carlton embraced his wife, wrapping her underneath the crook of his arm, as they lay against the plush, thousand thread count sheets. He nestled her closer and kissed her on the temple close to her hairline.

"You're such a good friend. Probably a better friend than any of the other housewives."

Meesha looked over at him. "I wouldn't say that. I think they're just as good-a-friends to me as I am to them. I mean, we all have our shortcomings and hang-ups. I'm the last one who can throw the spear at any of them."

"What about Avery?"

"What about her?" Meesha asked, shifting slightly so she could see her husband.

"Oh, nothing. I'm just saying, I talked to Ryker tonight. He was saying that she's been dealing with some issues since having their son. Postpartum depression from what he said."

"Yeah, she has, but she's getting better. She even seemed to have less of an attitude with me."

"Attitude with you?" Carlton eased up in the bed a bit, and looked down at Meesha. This was the first he'd heard of Avery having a problem with Meesha. She better not even think about saying anything to Meesha about their brief hit and run. The broad was looney and he was getting fed up with her foolish antics. "You've never mentioned this before. Why on earth would she have an attitude with you?"

"I didn't mention it because it's not worth mentioning. I mean, Avery, is Avery. She can get attitudish at times with all the ladies." Meesha shrugged. "I don't know why she acts like she hates me sometimes. Like I said, I guess it's just Avery being Avery. Even before she gave birth to RJ she had started treating me with a cool hand, but I didn't let it bother me then and I won't let it bother me now. It is what it is. Has she approached you about more counseling?"

Clearing his throat, Carlton responded, "Ummm, no...no she

hasn't." *She just better keep her mouth shut or she'll be sorry. Some of these women are crazy and I just happened to mess off with one that tops a lot of these fools out here.* "Enough talk about your friends. Whaddaya say we concentrate on you and me, Mrs. Porter."

"If you insist, Mr. Porter," Meesha cooed.

Carlton's hands slipped across her belly and her thighs. His mouth connected with hers as they started their own private party.

Chapter 22

"Trust not in him that seems a saint." *Thomas Fuller*

Her cell phone rang almost as soon as Avery got into her car after dropping Heather and Lexie off at school.

"Hi, there. What's up?"

'I…I need someone to talk to," Eva cried.

"Sure. What's wrong? Are you okay. Are you at school? You sound like you've been crying."

"Can I come over?" Eva asked, not answering Avery's line of questions.

"Uhhh, sure. I just dropped the girls off. I'm on my way home. You can meet me there in about twenty minutes."

"Thanks. I'll see you then."

The call went dead. Avery drove out of the school parking lot and headed home. She had planned to run a few errands, but from the sound of her friend's voice, she knew that she needed her. What could have happened? She hadn't talked to Eva since the night of Derek's surprise party. She thought everything was well. Harper had surprised Eva by showing up at the party, and it seemed like they had a good time. What possibly could have happened between then and now, four days later?

Eva stood in front of the bathroom mirror and made up her face. Harper was gone and for that she was grateful. He actually left early that morning to film several shows. From there, he was off on a month long book tour.

When he showed up at the party the other night, she was surprised. He had told her that he had emergency surgery, so she had no idea that he would be done in enough time to make an appearance. They spent the evening dancing, eating, talking to friends, and enjoying the birthday celebration. Harper was always good at socializing whether he was the host or the guest.

He mingled with people, many of which knew him already and didn't require official introductions. He spent time after they finished eating talking to Emma Winters and also to her grandsons. During the course of the evening, Harper, Derek, Ryker, and Carlton spent time huddled together laughing and talking, too.

When Quentin came back up to her and asked for a second dance, she looked out the side of her eye and saw Harper's accusing stare and politely excused herself from his presence, and hurriedly ran off to rejoin some other people she knew at the affair.

After the party ended and they were on their way home, he talked about the party and how much he enjoyed himself. Eva felt relaxed and relieved that he wasn't going to go off into one of his rampages. Everything was normal until they arrived home—that's when Lucifer himself showed up and all hell broke loose and he accused her of sleeping with Quentin. The more she denied it, the more he questioned her about how long she'd known him, how long they had been sleeping together, and on and on he went until the sun came up. She begged and pleaded for him to stop accusing her of things that were not true. They argued for hours until he finally relented, and practically ordered her to bed because they had to 'get ready for church' in a few hours.

Eva undressed, showered, and got into the bed while Harper did the same. When he exited the shower, she had given in to sleep. Her body and mind exhausted.

She had yet to divulge to Avery, or any of the housewives, about Harper's changed personality and abuse. Why would she when she was the one to blame for his erratic behavior? If only she had kept her legs closed and not given in to Seth.

The next morning, following the party, they got up, went to church, came home, and enjoyed a nice brunch together. He didn't mention anything else about their explosive argument. It was like the old Harper. The Harper who was gentle, kind, attentive, and loving. The next two days were also good days.

Yesterday is when things took an abrupt change. Eva had an enjoyable day at culinary school. She was learning more than she ever had about cooking utensils, knives, and all types of food. They made a meat dish, something that she would think would be relatively simple, yet was surprisingly detailed. She had envisioned attending school and jumping right into preparing food, but it wasn't like that. It was so much more to learn and she soaked in every piece of knowledge she could.

When she got home that afternoon, she showered, changed into some casual clothes, and chilled. Marissa had prepared dinner, as usual, and she had very little, if anything, to do.

She watched several shows on television well into the evening, and video chatted with her family in Bolivia, which always put a smile on her face and made her heart glad. After that she got prepared for bed. She had learned not to expect Harper until late at night—tonight was no different. She studied her culinary book for a couple of hours until sleepiness overtook her.

In her sleep, she dreamed about owning a chain of restaurants and saw herself traveling all over the world. There was a man in her dreams too. He had swept her off her feet and travelled the world with her. At first the face of the man wasn't visible, but just as she felt a deafening thud against her head, she saw the face of the man belonged to Quentin Winters.

Eva screamed as she was beaten awake by Harper. He accused her of having an affair with Quentin again. Another night of torment. She raised her hands to shield herself from his vicious blows across her semi-nude body. She wanted to get away, but she knew she had to stay.

Eva drove along the private drive leading to Avery's home. Once inside the foyer, she was met by Avery who had been waiting on her best friend's arrival with eager anticipation and worry.

"What's going on? Come on inside." She took Eva by the hand like she would Heather or Lexie and led her down the long, winding foyer and hallway to the far side of the house where there was a luxurious room with an expansive view of the beachfront.

"Sit down, take off your sunglasses. Relax. You sounded uptight over the phone. It scared me."

Eva slowly removed her sunglasses to a horrified Avery.

"Oh, my God. What happened? Were you in an accident?"

Tears poured out of Eva's blackened eyes and trailed down her face. *Silence.*

"Eva, talk to me. Tell me what happened? I asked you if you were in an accident."

Avery got up, exited the room, and returned with an opened box of tissues. She walked over to where Eva was and sat down next to her. She wrapped her arm around her friend. She was worried. What had happened? Why wouldn't Eva tell her what was going on?

"You know you can talk to me, Eva. You're my best friend. You can trust me." She pulled out a couple tissues and began wiping Eva's face. As she wiped away her tears, Eva's concealer came off on the tissue and Avery placed her hand over her mouth to stifle her own cries.

Eva cried even harder, and Avery pulled her to her bosom like she was one of the girls. She patted the back of her head. "Who did this to you? Please, Eva, talk to me." She pushed Eva away from her. Tears gathered in the corners of her own eyes at seeing Eva bruised and beaten.

"Harper."

"What did you say? Please tell me that you didn't tell me Harper did this? Why? I don't understand."

Eva used the tissue to dab at her own face and then she tearfully and shamefully confessed to Avery everything that had been going on over the past months.

Avery listened intently to every word, her anger fuming, and her disbelief mounting. Harper? Harper did this? He was capable of exacting this kind of violent, vile act on another human being when he had taken a vow as a doctor to save people's lives? No matter what she'd done, she didn't deserve this, no one did.

"Why are you still with him, Eva? Why? Did you call the police?"

"Haven't you heard anything I've said?" Eva retorted, trying not to be angry with Avery. She understood that Avery wanted what was best for her, but she didn't think Avery understood how much Eva stood to lose.

"Yes, and I understand that he's taking care of your family. I know you want to finish culinary school and try to set up your own restaurants so you can be self-sufficient, but my God, who says you'll be around to do that? If Harper is capable of doing something like this, God knows that the man could kill you in one of these fits of rage you say he goes into. You have to leave, Eva. You have to get as far away from him as you can."

"I left for a few days, got a suite at the Setai."

"And you went back? Why?"

"I couldn't stay there forever. It was on his account. He didn't say anything to me about it, but I knew that at any moment all he had to do was call the Setai and tell them to kick me out of there. I wasn't going to wait until that happened. I don't have any money saved. I trusted Harper and so I haven't put a dime aside. I should have been saving money whenever he gave it to me, but the truth is, he's never given me lots of cash. I mean, I always use a credit card for spending. And before you say it, I'll say it first--I'm estúpido. Stupid, stupid, stupid." She started crying again.

"You are *not* stupid. You were in love. You trusted him and you had no reason to believe things would end up like this. Listen, you can stay here in one of the guest rooms for as long as you like. And if it's money you need, I'll give you enough to get your own place or go to a hotel. Whatever you want to do."

"No, I can't do that, and I won't take your money. I have to go back. I have to do as he says until I can make things better for my parents."

"Oh, my God, this is unbelievable." Avery stood up and started pacing. "Is he still going out of town? I thought you told me he was going to do a tour for that new book of his."

"Yes, thank God he left this morning. He's supposed to be gone for a month."

"So, he did this to you before he left? Some parting gift, huh. You've got to talk to Ryker. He'll help you."

"No, please….you can't tell anyone, Avery. Please, I'm begging you. Not until I figure some things out. Let's talk about something else."

"Come on. Let's go for a walk in the garden."

"Yes, that would be great," Eva agreed. She stood up, and before Avery could reach the sliding doors leading to the outside, Eva was at the doors pushing them back.

They walked along the beautiful landscaped grounds.

"How are you coping with having a baby after all these years?" Eva asked.

"I'm good. I think I'm almost back to normal. I've been seeing my therapist, and she says I'm doing a hundred percent better. She didn't have to tell me that, I can feel that I am."

"Good for you. Have you given anymore thought about ruining your marriage to Ryker for that low down, sneaky, dressed up like an angel, Carlton Porter?" Eva felt her anger rising and she tried to calm herself down. Lately she had been like a different person and she knew that it was because she had been suppressing her own horrible secret about Harper's abuse. She was so glad that she had finally told Avery everything. It had been killing her to keep things to herself, but she had to be careful. Harper had already warned her about what he would do if she breathed a word to anyone about what was going on inside their marriage. She was not about to cross him again, but she needed Avery. She was the only one she could fully trust.

"I've decided that I'm going to try my best to keep my marriage intact. Ryker and I are finally in a good place, a real good place, and I don't want to do anything to jeopardize that. Anyway, this baby has his name and as far as I'm concerned, RJ is his kid. Yes, I'm heartbroken over how Carlton treated me, but I know God is in control of everything, and that all things work together for our good, but I just can't see any good that can come out of this situation for Carlton, not in the long run at least. I'm trying to move forward with my life. You were right, Eva. I have too much to lose. If Ryker ever found out about Carlton and me he would get my kids and leave me with nothing. I can't take that chance, no matter how much I love Carlton."

"Then you should understand the situation I'm in. It may not involve children, but it's my family."

"Oh, Eva," Avery said. She stopped walking and embraced her friend. "I do understand, sweetie. I really do, but Ryker is not a violent man. Look at what Harper has done to you. I'm afraid for you."

"Don't be. I'll be okay. I'm glad you're going to accept that RJ is Ryker's. Let things stay the way they are."

"The baby *is* Ryker's"

"How do you know that for sure?"

"I did one of those over the counter DNA tests."

"How did you get Ryker to agree to that?"

"Let's just say I had my ways and it worked out just as I planned."

"Are you sure it's Ryker's child?"

"Ninety-nine point nine nine percent sure," Avery said, smiling as they started walking again.

Chapter 23

"Before you give up, think about why you held on for so long." Unknown

Derek moved back into their bedroom the night of his surprise birthday party. Words could not describe how happy it made Peyton. Her taste for vodka had basically left and she couldn't see herself ever going back to the old Peyton Hudson.

She began to see just how much she'd lost out on when she was nothing more than a rich drunk, and she didn't want to experience that side of her anymore. She and Liam's relationship was improving everyday, too. That was another blessing.

Derek took her to the orthopedic doctor and she left the doctor's office ecstatic that she no longer had to wear the mobilizers. She couldn't go back to wearing heels just yet, but she could wear her own shoes.

"So what other plans do you have today?" Derek asked as they drove from her doctor's appointment.

"Me and the other housewives are having our ladies' day out. I thought that we would meet at our house."

Derek continued to focus on the road ahead. "Sounds good. After I drop you off, I'm going to the office. I have a busy schedule today, but I should be home in time for us to go to

Liam's game."

"Okay, sweetheart."

The car got quiet and Peyton looked over at her husband.

"What is it?" Derek asked.

"Since you've moved back into our bedroom, does that mean we have a chance of salvaging our marriage?"

Derek paused as if in deep thought. "I love you, Peyton. I always have. But we've been through some tough times, real tough times. I don't have to remind you that your drinking caused a lot of the problems between us, and then the situation with Liam…that was a real shocker, too. It's like you have never trusted me. We've been together for fifteen years, and you still lie and keep things from me."

Derek was telling the truth, and Peyton couldn't deny it. She squirmed in her seat as Derek continued the drive home. What could she say?

"Look, you're right. You're right about everything. I've been a terrible wife and a bad mother. I've lied, kept secrets from you, and cut you down throughout our marriage. I've made you feel less than a man and doubted you every step of the way, even though you're a brilliant and successful man, not to mention a good human being. So why would you want to work out this marriage?"

"Yeah, why would I?" Derek replied, glancing over at her briefly before refocusing on the road.

"Because, like you said, you love me. And believe it or not, I love you, too, Derek. I always have, and I want our marriage to work. I want our family back together. I know that I will never take another drink again and I will never belittle you ever again. I'll keep seeing the therapist if that's what you want."

"It's not what *I* want, it should be what *you* want, Peyton. Do this for yourself and for our son."

"I will. I promise you, Derek. Just say you'll give us another chance."

Derek reached over and squeezed her hand tenderly, but said nothing as they entered through the gate leading to their estate. He didn't know why it made him uneasy whenever Peyton approached the subject of them getting back together. Why couldn't she just allow things to happen naturally? For one, he had been living in the other side of the house since he and Liam came back home—until now. He moved out of the house with Liam, leaving Peyton for a time, because he couldn't deal with her lies and her drinking anymore. If he had stayed away, he would stand a chance at Liam hating his mother forever. He didn't want Liam to have to deal with two parents at odds all the time. The boy already felt it was because of him that he and Peyton's marriage had hit a snag. But it wasn't because of their son, it was because Peyton chose to keep the truth from him about Liam's birth mother, about Carlton Porter, about how she got Liam…about everything. Add drinking nonstop to that equation and their marriage was a recipe for failure. Peyton's accident changed all of that, too. He returned home after she almost killed herself and those two cops.

Yet, he couldn't shake her, couldn't shake the hold she had on him. He loved her and he returned home. It wasn't out of pity, not really, but he wasn't the kind of man that could turn himself away from someone who needed him, and his wife needed him.

He still was uncertain how long Peyton would stay away from the alcohol. During the fifteen years they had been married there were times in the past when she'd stopped drinking. One time she stopped for an entire year only to go right back to the vodka bottle without any explanation. He was afraid that the same thing would happen again. It was likely that it would. It had been a little less than a year since she plowed down those two police officers. Yeah, so far she had adhered to everything that the court ordered. Thanks to Ryker's expert defense, she'd gotten off with a light penalty. Considering the DUI and the accident, it could have been so much worse. She could have served a long stint in jail but instead she did a few weeks of house arrest, was placed on probation, and paid the courts and the officers a pretty hefty fine in exchange for her freedom. He thought about people who didn't have the money or means to fight such cases and sometimes it made him angry that people like Peyton who abused the law could pay their way to freedom.

Derek admitted to himself that he and Peyton had seen some tough times and yet they were still together. He had been raised and taught early on that marriage was sacred and that no one belonged in it other than the couple married to one another. It wasn't that he was such a good man, not in his own eyesight, because he had his own issues. He loved money for one thing. Growing up with very little of it, when he met Peyton and her family, they gave him a leg up and then the development of the App gave him the type of financial freedom he could only once dream about. He still pinched himself from time to time, amazed at his blessings and good fortune. He would spend hours upon hours devising ways to make more money. The more he made the more he wanted and needed. He would let nothing stand in the way of that.

Now that Peyton had come out and asked him directly about saving their marriage, he had nothing to say. It was as if he clammed up. He didn't want to give her false hope. He wanted to take things one day at a time, because only time would tell if she was a changed person like she professed. He saw the evidence. He saw how much better things were between her and their son, and that surprise birthday party, it was one of the best nights of his life. She had really outdone herself with that, but was it enough for them to move forward? Then there was the fact that she had never been able to give him a child. He loved Liam like he was his own flesh and blood son, but deep inside he often longed for a child of his own—one that had been created from his sperm, but for some reason it never happened for them. Peyton was thirty-seven years old, and though it wasn't impossible, and because it had not happened so far, he believed it was doubtful that she would ever get pregnant, and he had come to accept that. It was a portion of him that blamed her drinking for her not getting pregnant. He had no proof of that, but he secretly believed that she was the cause of her own infertility. Time would have to tell if their marriage would survive.

Chapter 24

"It is better to break your own heart by leaving, rather than having that person break your heart every day you're with them." Unknown

Eva parked, got out of the car, and headed to class after she dropped the dogs off at the groomer. She would pick them up after she finished class.

She felt exhilarated and free since Harper was still out of town. He would call her ever so often, and that was fine with her. When he told her that four states had been added to his tour, she couldn't have been happier. That meant he would be gone an additional two weeks. If she never heard from him again, that would be even better but she needed his money, his influence, and in a crazy sort of way, she needed his power.

Culinary class went smoothly. It was another enjoyable day. The class had begun preparing more simple dishes, and Eva loved it. At the end of class, she lingered and talked with her instructor before leaving for the afternoon. She climbed inside her car, gave the groomers a call to see if the dogs were ready, and then turned the ignition. A knock against her window startled her. It was *him*.

"Hi. How are you?" Quentin asked when she pushed the

power button for the window to go down.

"I'm good. How are you?" she asked. She didn't know if a smile was plastered on her face or not. She felt like there was because she felt a warm glow flow through her.

"I haven't seen you since the party."

"I could say the same for you," she replied.

His smile was always dashing. "I guess you could. I've been looking for you."

"I've been here everyday. Monday through Thursday," she said.

"Is that right?"

"Yes, that's right," she responded.

"Would you like to go have a cup of coffee…lunch?" he asked, leaning down in the car.

His cologne was intoxicating. "Sorry, I can't. I have to go pick up my dogs from the groomer, but thanks for the invite."

"What about later? We can have dinner."

"You do recall that I am a married woman, don't you?"

"Yes, I know you're married—to Dr. Harper Stenberg, I think," he said and laughed. "I respect that. I just thought we'd go, learn a little about each other, strictly as friends. No strings attached."

"Maybe some other time," she said. "I really need to go. It was nice seeing you, Quentin." She put the car in Reverse.

"Hold up."

"Yes?"

"Take my number."

"Why would I do that?"

"Come on, don't give a brother a hard time. If you find yourself free and you want to talk or hang out, then give me a call. Plus, I want to talk to you about volunteering at the rescue shelter."

Eva smiled and looked over her shoulder and across the street at Quentin's store.

"Volunteer?"

"Yes, see the sign in the window?"

Sure enough, there was a sign in the picture window that read *Volunteers Needed. Only Animal Lovers Need Apply.*

"Ummm, Okay, I'll take your number," she said while putting the car in Park, and removing her cell phone to enter his phone number into her Contacts.

"What days and hours?" she asked.

"It's flexible. We just need committed volunteers. People who have a heart for animals."

"Okay, I'll think about it. Now, really, I have to go."

Quentin stepped back and away from the car. "Take care, Eva."

Eva blushed, backed out of the parking space, and maneuvered the car into the busy street.

Quentin walked back toward his establishment. He had found out some things about Eva and Harper through his grandmother that gave him hope. Emma Winters told him everything wasn't coming up roses like Harper Stenberg expected when he married Eva. She told him about the time he threw Eva out of the house.

Harper had been confiding in Emma Winters for quite some time. He found her to be like his deceased grandmother, energetic, full of life, and Godly wisdom. He gravitated toward the woman when he was troubled or needed advice about a situation. Discussing his struggling marriage with Emma was no exception.

Quentin was intrigued by Eva. He didn't want to break up a happy home, but if the home wasn't happy then he might as well try to bring a little joy into Eva Stenberg's life. He and Harper were not friends, they were more like acquaintances. They traveled in some of the same circles, but Quentin's scope of friends included other real estate investors, animal activists, and the restaurant world. He was more acquainted with Harper because of his grandmother, who adored Harper for some reason.

Quentin thought it might have been because his grandmother often said Harper reminded her of Quentin's father, her only son.

Emma's husband died some years back, so it was just her and her two grandsons. She was overjoyed when Quentin made the decision to move back to Adverse City to help take care of her. She was spry and able to do for herself and get around, but she welcomed the company of her grandson, since her other grandson was now married and trying to start a family of his own. It was a tragic day and time when their parents were killed. Emma still grieved for her son though it had been twenty plus years since his and her daughter-in-law's deaths.

Quentin was a thirty-five year old single, successful biracial male with no kids, but he wasn't the kind of guy that bedded women for mere pleasure. He liked long-term relationships, getting to know a woman, and spending time with her. He had never been much of the playboy type. His grandmother had taught him better. He casually walked back across the street, confident that he would hear from her again.

Her cell phone rang. "Yes, Harper."

"Where are you?" he asked without acknowledging her salutation.

"Where I am everyday at this time—leaving school."

"I'm not sure exactly when I'll be back. The tour is going so well that they keep adding tour sites. And we're even doing some filming for the television show. It's great."

Eva said nothing but a big smile came across her face at hearing that Harper wouldn't be home at his original date.

"Are you there?"

"Uh, yes, I'm here," she said. "Glad your tour is going well. Look, I'm driving, Harper. Is that all you wanted to tell me?" she asked coldly. She was sick of pretending that all was well between them when it was like pure torture everyday she remained Mrs. Harper Stenberg. It was bad enough she had to put on a smiling face in public so behind closed doors she wasn't going to pretend any longer.

"I'll call or video chat with you tomorrow."

"Sure. Whatever."

"Goodbye, sweetheart," he said and ended the call.

She waited to see his call disappear from her dash and breathed a heavy sigh of welcome relief. As she drove toward home, she thought about Quentin's offer. She *could* consider volunteering at his store. What harm could it do? Then again, if Harper found out, she knew what the backlash would be and it wouldn't be pretty. She couldn't take any more beatings, but would he even have to know?

She loved animals and maybe she could bring her dogs to the shelter sometimes, too. They were mild mannered dogs and would probably get along fine with some of the rescues. She would think about it a little longer and if she still felt the same later this evening then she would call Quentin and let him know she wanted to sign up. *Maybe I should tell Harper. But if he beat me for dancing with Quentin....* Eva shuttered at the thought.

Harper used to tell her she needed to get a hobby, so this would be the perfect thing. She had long since stopped volunteering at Perfecting Your Faith Ministries since she had the pregnancy scare. Now that she knew Carlton was a charlatan, she surely wasn't interested in being anywhere that could bring her into his deceitful presence. Poor Meesha. If only she knew who she was married to then she would have hurried to the divorce courts when he was begging to get out of their marriage.

Eva thought about Meesha and questioned whether she was a true friend to Meesha or not. Knowing that Carlton was a cheat, should she have told Meesha what she knew about him. But if she did, then that would mean she would have to spill the beans on his and Avery's affair. That was the last thing she wanted to do. No way would she ever betray Avery's trust. Avery had been taken full advantage of by Carlton. She was a helpless victim. Someway, somehow, he had to get what was due him. Just like

Harper had to pay the piper, Carlton had to stand in that same line. If only she could devise a way to bring them both down.

Chapter 25

"My worst enemy is my MEMORY." Unknown

Meesha didn't know what caused the nightmares to resurface. At least once or twice a week, Carlton woke her up out of her sleep, telling her that she was screaming and talking unintelligibly.

It frightened Meesha because the last thing she wanted was to say something in her sleep that would cause Carlton suspicion. She didn't need him to start questioning her about her past. She tried to explain the night dreams away by telling him that she was stressed from working at the Academy, seeing to the kids, and being a dutiful first lady and wife. She was exhausted mentally and physically, she explained.

Carlton seemed to buy her excuse and insisted that she back up from the obligations and duties she fulfilled at Perfecting Your Faith Academy, rely more on their nanny, and tailor her duties as First Lady. She reluctantly agreed. She loved the school, and enjoyed being its administrator. It gave her a life outside of her family. It was rewarding work that she believed God had called her to do, but if putting it on pause would help alleviate mental stress and make the dreams stop, then she was all for it. Nothing was worth losing her peace of mind over.

If only there was someone she could talk to, confide in about her sordid, wicked past, but there was no one…no one but God. Lately, Meesha felt that even God seemed to be growing tired of her pleas and she didn't know what she would do. So many things had happened that had her mind going in a thousand different directions. From the trouble she had experienced in her marriage, to the death of that poor woman, Breyonna, to giving birth to her fifth child, and the list went on.

She drove the short distance, parked, got out of her car, and walked along the beach thinking about her life and thanking God for bringing her to Adverse City where she could have a new start.

Meesha thought often of that murderous night. She had even tried a time or two to look up some of Terrell's family members on social media. She wasn't too successful with that, but she did find Cash on social media, the guy Catherine had been dating during that time but she didn't reach out to him. There was no reason to. She searched for Catherine too, but she didn't find her. It could have been that Catherine had gotten married and her last name was changed. Meesha didn't know and she didn't put any more thought into resurrecting that part of her past—a shameful past, that if found out, could take her away from her family, her children, and land her behind bars for years.

"You have a collect call from an inmate…" the robotic caller stated. "Press One to accept or Two to disconnect."

Carlton pressed the number one on his keypad.

"Hello, what's up partner?" the voice on the other end said.

"Klay, my man," Carlton said, always happy to hear from his best friend. Having to be locked away for years didn't change the fact that Carlton and Klay were like brothers. Carlton continued to make sure he was more than well provided for while in prison.

"How's it going?" Klay asked.

"Things are good. Meesha had the baby."

"Another nappy headed boy?" Klay teased.

"Man, Klay. I got a girl. Can you believe it? After four tries, I have a beautiful little princess." Carlton almost teared up at the thought, but didn't.

"Whooooa, I can't believe it. Congratulations, bruh. Man, I'm happy for you and Meesha. I take it things are continuing to go well for the two of you."

"Yeah. Things are good. You know I told you the last time we talked that things were pretty much back on track. I'm grateful to God…and to you."

"Look, you coming up anytime soon?" Klay quickly shifted the conversation. Nothing was secure or safe on the jailhouse lines. Sometimes it seemed like Carlton forgot that and Klay would have to pull him back in to keep things that were private, private.

"I plan on taking that drive in a few days to see you, man. Kingston and Martin are supposed to be riding with me."

"Cool, I'll be looking forward to that visit. It's been a minute since I've seen them."

"Anything you need?" Carlton asked.

'Yeah, as a matter of fact there is. That is, if you can make it happen again."

"You know where there's a will there's a way."

"In that case, see if you can arrange a visit again. Your bruh needs some one-on-one counseling," Klay said.

"You got it. A private counseling session will be arranged," Carlton told him.

"You have twenty seconds," the robotic voice interrupted as they talked.

"I'll see you in a few days, partner. And be looking to hear about that private session. I'll make the call as soon as we hang up," Carlton reassured him.

"See you, bruh," Klay said. "And thanks."

"I owe all the thanks to you. You saved my life…and my

marriage," Carlton was able to say just as the call came to an end.

As promised, Carlton made the usual phone call and spoke to Phyllis Wade. She was a longtime friend from back in the day too, the same as Klay. She worked inside the prison system as a psychologist and could make things happen that were otherwise unattainable. A conjugal visit with an unsuspecting female was one of those things.

"Okay, but this time you owe me a juicy steak dinner," Phyllis told Carlton as they laughed over the phone.

"You got it. I'll even buy your husband one, too," Carlton promised and chuckled loudly.

The two friends chatted for a while before ending the call and Carlton returned to his pastorly duties. While he completed some paperwork, he thought back to Breyonna's timely death. *Thank you God for friends in high places. Rest in peace, Breyonna. Avery Mitchelson, you better not cross me. You won't like me if you cross me.*

As he promised, Carlton made the trip to see his best friend. Kingston and Martin couldn't make the visit with him after all. Damica had made an appointment for their cake tasting and no way could Kingston back out of that. He had been drilled by his married friends, including Carlton, that a happy wife meant a happy life, and he was starting out ahead of his marriage by doing things to make his bride-to-be keep a smile on her face.

Martin had committed to attending an outing sponsored by Perfecting Your Faith. He and a team of volunteers, along with his wife and two kids, were taking a group of kids from one of the inner-city youth ministries operated by Perfecting Your Faith Ministries on a two-day weekend trip to Disney World. Martin was good at planning things like that, and it made Carlton proud of the man his brother was.

Carlton played music from his playlist and listened to sermons by fellow pastors on the three-hour drive to the prison. His cell phone rang along the way. He looked at the dash and saw a familiar number. "Hey you," he said.

"Hey, what you up to?" the sweet, seductive sounding voice asked.

"On the road," he said, smiling as he pushed ninety miles per hour on the highway in his Bentley.

"You didn't tell me you were coming to see me," she said and giggled into the phone.

Carlton laughed too. "Not this time. I have a friend that I'm on my way to see. Like I told you, we have to be discreet…very discreet. You have a husband and I have a wife. We don't want to do anything to mess up our happy homes now do we?

"Right you are, but I miss you, Carlton," the mysterious woman said.

"I thought you were going to be unavailable this weekend."

"Yeah, me too, but things changed."

"Should have called me earlier. You could have made the trip with me. I would have gotten us a hotel, went to visit my friend, and then came back… after that I would have been all yours. You could have had your way with me," Carlton flirted.

"Yeah, I wasn't thinking."

Carlton's car dash showed Meesha calling him. "Look, I have to hang up. I'll hit you up later this evening. I'll call you when I'm headed back to the city. Maybe we can meet at our spot around eight or nine."

"Okay, baby. Bye."

Carlton ended the call and quickly clicked over to Meesha. "Hey, love. How's it going?"

Chapter 26

"If you haven't any kind of charity in your heart, you have the worst heart trouble." Bob Hope

Eva made the decision to take the chance and volunteer at Quentin's store, hoping against hope that Harper would not discover what she was doing. It was risky stepping out and going behind his back, but she decided to do it nonetheless. It gave her something else meaningful to do with her time and kept her away from the house. For now, things were working perfectly, with Harper being away. She refused to think of what would happen if he ever discovered what she was doing.

Volunteering at the shelter was proving to be fun and exciting just as she'd hoped. There was always something going on that kept her on her toes. Some days brought tears to her eyes when she accompanied Quentin on rescues of abused and injured animals. It was hard to fathom how cruel a human being could be toward an animal, but then she thought about how cruel Harper was to her. He treated her like she was an animal. It was heartbreaking, but Quentin had such a gentle way with the animals. Eva could see in the way he treated the animals that he genuinely cared about their wellbeing. She admired that about him.

Eva didn't attend school on Fridays or the weekends so she

spent as many hours as she could at the shelter. She had fallen in love with the giant weimeraner, Scooby Doo looking dog. He was just a big baby and he seemed to adore her. Quentin had been right, the dog wouldn't scratch a flea. He was just a big loveable, oversized canine who craved affection and attention.

Quentin looked forward to seeing Eva walk into the shelter. She was quickly becoming his *go to* person. She had learned a great deal about the different breeds of canines and felines. She loved to show them affection and she had learned a lot about grooming them and even started some minor training of the animals.

"I still can't get over how that poor cocker spaniel was abused and left for dead," Eva said after they had returned from a rescue call Quentin received one afternoon soon after she arrived at the shelter.

"You can't imagine some of the cases I've had. I want to save as many of these poor animals as I possibly can. My parents were animal lovers and rescued animals when I was a little boy. They often took my brother me and along on their rescue missions. It's why I do what I do. It's been instilled inside of me. You know?"

"I'm learning so much. Thank you for letting me be part of this experience, Quentin."

"Thank you for volunteering. Most of our volunteers are college students so I don't have them for very many hours. You've been the biggest help and I appreciate you."

Eva transported many of the animals, when needed, in the company van. She was exactly the kind of woman he would want as a companion. Someone who had a love and concern for animals as much or even more than he did.

"Would you like to get a bite to eat?" he asked her one Friday afternoon after they finished up at the shelter earlier than usual.

Eva wanted to tell him yes, but Harper was supposed to be home later that evening and she didn't want to do anything that would cause him to catch an attitude or give him suspicion about where she was and what she was doing. She shuttered at the thought of another merciless beating at his hands.

"We can go to one of the restaurants across the street on the strip," he said, "and celebrate our rescue of those cats and dogs from that abandoned house."

She thought about it. What could it hurt? It was just past one o'clock and Harper wasn't due in until at least eight o'clock. She accepted his offer and they went to lunch.

"I want you to know that you are a huge part of the rescue team, Eva. I'm so glad you came along. You're the best help I have. I mean that. I should put you on payroll but I wouldn't want to insult you," he complimented as he sat across the table from her staring into her eyes.

He smiled and she felt her heart melting. She would love to be on somebody's payroll. That way she could save money without Harper knowing. "Are you serious?" she asked as they ate their sandwiches.

"Serious about what? Putting you on payroll?" he looked curiously at her.

"Yes."

"Like I said, I wouldn't insult you like that."

"What if I told you it wouldn't be an insult?"

He looked at her strangely and thought about what his grandmother had told him about Eva's troubled marriage. Peering into her soft eyes he could see she was serious. She looked almost as if she was pleading with him to help her.

"Look, can I be honest with you?"

"Yeah, you can." Quentin responded.

"If you're going to run back and tell Harper then let me know now. But I want to—"

"Stop. Stop right there," Quentin said. Reaching across the table that separated them, he took one of her hands and held it in his.

Eva felt a bolt of electricity rush through her. She looked at his hand holding hers and then looked up and into his eyes.

"Let's get something straight right now. I don't betray my friends, and we are friends. At least, I consider us friends. Do you?"

"Yes," she said, pausing.

"Okay, then believe it or not, I'm a trustworthy guy, Eva. If you tell me something, it goes no farther. As for your husband, Harper is my grandmother's friend, not mine. We're acquaintances strictly because of his relationship with her. My grandmother is also a woman of integrity. She is not a gossip or an instigator, and she taught me and my brother well, know what I mean?"

Eva nodded.

His voice dropped in volume as he said, "It may take you some time, but you'll find out that you *can* trust me, Eva." He looked deep into her eyes and he felt like she was holding a lot of hurt and pain back. He didn't know how bad her marriage was, but something told him there was more to Eva Stenberg than what meets the eye.

Eva inhaled deeply and then slowly released a long sigh before she began to speak. "Harper doesn't know that I'm volunteering at your shelter. I would like to keep it that way. If he finds out then he would be upset, and I do not want to upset my husband." She paused, pinched her lower lip with her teeth, then proceeded to speak slowly, almost cautiously. "Next, I would like to make my own money. I haven't made money of my own since I left Bolivia four years ago."

"Say no more. I'd like to offer you the position as my right hand man, or should I say, right hand woman." He laughed, hoping to lighten up the seriousness of what he heard her say.

"Your right hand woman?" Her eyebrows rose in obvious pleasure. "What exactly does that mean?" she replied, smiling while putting a bite of food inside her mouth.

"I need a part-time assistant director for the store and shelter. I've been actively looking for someone like you who understands animals and with the same mindset as I have when it comes to doing whatever possible to protect and care for them. Since Lisa has to return to college in a few weeks, you'll be the perfect person to take her place. She'll only be able to work at the store a few hours in the evening twice a week, as part of her work-study. You're here far more than she is already. It'll be perfect. I'm willing to pay you handsomely for your time, and I'm willing to work around your hours. If Harper demands your time and you are unable to come in, then I'll understand. Your schedule will be totally flexible…and I promise, mum's the word. Scout's honor," he said, smiling while he displayed the two-finger Scout sign.

He saw her eyes grow large with excitement. He could tell she must have really needed the money for whatever reason. He suspected she was in some type of marital trouble probably far worse than his grandmother had told him. He wanted to do whatever he could to help her.

Quentin was attracted to her that he couldn't deny. She was not only beautiful, she was different than many of the women he had dated, and he had dated women from all over the world because of his businesses. Eva was demure, shy like, and he could tell she was the kind of woman that would be easy to love. What she had going on in her marriage, he didn't know, and he wasn't the kind of fellow who wanted to cause a rift in anyone's relationship, whether it was a marriage or a courtship. However with her, and the way she caused his desire to peak, he hoped he would be able to control his urges. He imagined taking her into his arms, holding her, kissing her, and making love to her over and over again. Knowing that wasn't possible, the only thing he could do since she was a taken woman, was to be as good a friend to her as he possibly could. "So, what do you say?"

"It's more than I could ever ask, Quentin."

"So, what's the answer?"

"I say, meet your new assistant director, Mr. Winters." She extended her manicured hand toward his and he gladly accepted it, kissed the back of it, and gave her that deep, sensual dynamite smile of his.

"One more thing," she said, laughing.

"What is that?" Quentin responded with a grin on his face.

"Were you really a boy scout?"

Chapter 21

Carlton made the drive to Coleman, Florida to see Klay. Everything was as he planned. He had already made his monthly deposit into Klay's account so his best friend could live the best life possible considering he was behind bars. Carlton spoke to Ryker while they were at Derek's birthday party about Klay. He wanted to do everything he could to get the case retried with the reason being that Klay was temporarily insane at the time he committed murder. Ryker had heard of the case from Carlton once before, but that had been some time ago, and they hadn't talked seriously about it at the time.

After listening to Carlton, Ryker wasn't sure if there was justification for reopening the case and petitioning the court for a new trial, but he promised Carlton that he would look into it and if there was anything he could do, then he would.

"How are things going?" Carlton asked his best friend.

"It's going as well as it can you know, being locked up. I'm glad I have much more freedom than some of these other cats in here" Klay said. "Being a master electrician has proven to have its perks."

"Yeah, I know. You're not actually tied down to one place. They send you to different prisons and jails, and that's almost unheard of."

"Yeah, it's called cheap labor," Klay said and the two of them laughed as they sat across from each other in the controlled visitation area. The good thing was Klay didn't have to receive visitors from behind bars. He'd been deemed a low risk in spite of his brutal crime so he was able to sit out in the open with other prisoners and their loved ones who came to visit.

"Everything still straight?" Klay asked.

"Yeah. They closed the case."

"Good for you," Klay said. "What about that kid? Is he yours?"

"I thought I told you. No, turned out that broad was lying. Don't know who the heck his daddy is, and it's not my concern, but I went and got myself messed up with this other crazy woman."

"Man, that's all you attract, ain't it?" Klay said, jokingly.

"Looks like it. Anyway, she's one of Meesha's friends. We messed around a couple of times, now she's got a kid and she's trying to pin it on me. Not."

"Man, you need to wrap it up. You're too old for this kind of crap. You know you've never been able to stay faithful to one broad, so do like you gone tell your sons to do, keep that umbrella on. In your positon, you can't afford to blow in the wind. Know what I mean?"

"Yeah. I hear you and you're right. But you know me, when it's given to me on a silver platter when I least expect it, I can't say no." Carlton laughed.

"You handling her or nah?" Klay asked.

"Yeah, I made it clear that she better not cross me. She's backed off and she's married with kids so she has just as much to lose as I do."

"Bruh, you got to be more careful." Klay leaned back in his

steel chair and chuckled. "What about me? You got me that hook-up yet?"

"Do I even have to answer that?"

"No, just tell me when."

"I can't say, but just know in the next week or two you're going to get a lot of tension relieved. Believe that."

The two men fist bumped each other, talked some more until it was time for the visit to end.

They stood, gave each other dap. 'I'll see you next month," Carlton said. "Maybe next time I can get those two knuckle head brothers of mine to come. Kingston's nose is wide opened so he's doing everything his gal tells him to do so she won't leave him at the altar." Carlton and Klay laughed. "Martin is still being Martin. He's wrapped up in the church and with his family much like me, except I think he's a one woman man."

"Yeah, that's definitely not like you," Klay said and chuckled. "Good to see you, bruh. I appreciate everything you do to keep me straight in here. I love you, man."

"I love you. And seriously, putting all the bull aside, you know that I'm praying for you always, man.

"Yeah, I know. Take it light, and remember what I said. Strap up."

"I gotcha."

Carlton exited the prison. When he got inside his car, he made the phone call. "I'm on my way back to the city. You still straight with getting out?" he asked the female he spoke to earlier.

"Yeah, what time?"

"What about seven thirty? I won't go home. I'll call and tell Meesha something came up and I'm going to have to stay where I am overnight. I'll stop in Miami and get a room at our usual spot. You sure you can get out?"

"Yes, my weekend is free. I told Martin I changed my mind about going on the trip. I told him I wanted to chill, take advantage of the house being quiet without the kids. He was cool with that. That's why I called you earlier. I wanted to see you and I knew this would be the perfect weekend. One thing about my husband, I don't have to worry about him constantly ringing my phone. He's going to be too busy anyway. I told him if anything came up, I would call him. So, I'm good to go. You *can* always come over here, you know?"

"No way. That's too close for comfort. I'll see you at the same place. Seven thirty."

"Okay, bye, love. I can't wait to see you."

Carlton ended the call and then spoke into his phone and told it to call the Hilton Miami. He made the room reservations and next he called Meesha.

"Hey, sweetheart," he said.

"Hi. You on your way home?"

"No, that's why I was calling. I'm going to spend the night in Coleman. I want to see Klay again tomorrow. He's going to be shipped out for a few months to some other prison on some big electrical project. Since I'm up here, I told him I would come back. Is that okay with you?"

"Yeah, sure. How is he doing?" she asked.

"He's good. The kids and my little princess doing okay?"

"Yes. Makena is in my arms as we speak. The nanny took the boys for ice cream. They'll be back in an hour or so."

"Okay, well, I gotta go. I'm going to find a hotel. I'll call you later when I get settled."

"Okay, get some rest. We'll see you tomorrow," Meesha said.

"Yeah, tomorrow. Love you."

"I love you too, Carlton."

Carlton and Martin's wife had been seeing each other on and off for two and half years. She was his knock off and he was hers. That much was understood. What he liked about her was that she didn't want to mess up her marriage any more than he wanted to mess up his. She was nothing like crazy Avery. He thanked God that he had gotten her out of his life. All he had to do was make sure she kept her big mouth shut and not step to him about that kid of hers being his. He was glad he didn't have that concern with Evelyn. Evelyn loved Martin but like Carlton, one man was never enough for her. They saw each other whenever they could, neither demanding anything more than good sex from one another without commitment.

Carlton made the drive back to Miami in well under three hours. He always had a just in case bag packed in his trunk with a change of clothes and toiletries. He never knew what could happen when he traveled on the road in his car. He was always prepared for whatever came up. He checked into the hotel, took a shower, and started to get a bite to eat. He changed his mind about that and decided he would wait on Evelyn to come and they could grab something together.

"Hey, I'm here," he said after he got out of the shower and called his wife.

"Good, have you eaten?" Meesha asked.

"I'm about to do that now and then I'm going to call it a night. I'm beat," He did a fake yawn into the phone loud enough for her to hear.

"Okay, have a good night. I'll see you tomorrow."

Immediately after ending his call with Meesha, his phone rang. "I should be there in half an hour."

"Have you had dinner?" Carlton asked.

"No, I had a bite earlier."

"Okay, we'll order room service when you get here."

"Okay. I'll see you soon."

"See ya."

He turned on the radio in the room. Carlton smiled when he heard the song by Ella James. *"Summertime and the living is easy..."* He sat in the plush leather reclining chair, laid back so his legs were stretched out, then reached for the shot of bourbon sitting next to him on the table. He took a sip and smiled.

Chapter 28

"Good friends help you find the important things when you have lost them: Your smile, Your hope, Your courage." Homean quotes

Two months had passed since the ladies gathered for their last ladies' day out. Peyton was walking almost normal again although she still had some limited mobility. She experienced pain in her ankles from time to time but she had not returned to the bottle to nurse her wounds.

Her relationship with Derek was almost as if they were newlyweds. A smile was plastered on her face almost every time anyone saw Peyton. She and Liam's relationship was practically fully restored. Things were looking up for her and she couldn't have been more grateful.

Eva remained busy with school and trying to keep her mind off the trauma she suffered at the hands of Harper. He had recently returned from his book tour and remained busier than ever. This couldn't have worked out any better for Eva. She and Harper rarely saw one another, except on occasions late at night or in passing. It was almost as if she lived in their huge house all alone. He hadn't struck her since he returned from on the road, another blessing for Eva, and as far as she could tell, he hadn't discovered that she was working for Quentin Winters.

True to his word, Quentin paid her a generous salary for the few hours she worked at the shelter. No one had to tell her it was because he suspected that she really needed the money. She made sure she worked hard and did her best to show her gratitude for him giving her the chance to put money away. Plus, she loved working with the animals and next to him.

Knowing she could end up in a world of trouble, she occasionally had lunch and there was one other time she had dinner with Quentin after they had a long day rescuing animals. They had a fabulous time laughing and talking. She told him about her dreams to become a master chef and own her own restaurant. She learned so much from him about the restaurant business and how to achieve her dreams. He even promised to help her in any way he could once she finished school. Everything he shared with her she soaked up, eager to learn as much as possible for her own restaurant one day. He was pleasant and kind. He hadn't tried to push up on her, and for that she grew to respect and like him even more. Still she told herself to be extra careful and not take anything for granted. She couldn't chance Harper finding out what she was doing and going to that dark, dangerous place. Anything to keep the peace is what she told herself she needed to do when it came to Harper, while she carefully developed her plan.

Meesha's cell phone rang. She smiled when she saw the familiar face displayed on her screen. "Hey, what's up, Peyton?"

"Girl, too much to tell over this phone. Why don't I see if I can get in touch with Eva and Avery. Maybe we can have an impromptu ladies' day out. I'm about to go stir crazy up in this big ole house by myself."

"I feel ya. I'm at the beach with the boys right now. I had to have some time out of the house. I would like to see everyone, too. We haven't talked, I mean really talked, in what seems like ages. Other than at church, but that doesn't count."

"Yeah, we can't do our gossip thing or find out what's going on with each other when we're in church," Peyton agreed.

"You got that right. I guess each of us has had some kind of drama going on in our lives."

"Yes, I know for a fact that Eva is a train wreck. I can tell something is going on with her, probably Harper and his always busy schedule, but she'll have to fill us in on that situation—that is if she wants to talk about it. Anyway, I'll send out a group text and see what Eva and Avery are up to."

"Okay, bye, Peyton. Talk to you later."

`Impromptu ladies' day out. Are you ladies available for a late lunch today. Around 1 or 1:30?` texted Peyton to all of the housewives.

Each of them responded with a `"Yes."` They agreed to meet at Peyton's house.

Peyton got her personal chef to prepare veggie wraps, salad fixings, chips, salsa, and a gallon of lemon-iced tea. The chef made non-bake, nondairy, peanut fudge brownies for dessert.

Peyton had everything set up in the backyard around the outside kitchen. She was beginning to enjoy entertaining.

When the ladies arrived, the chef remained in the outside kitchen preparing fun, colorful non-alcoholic drinks. The ladies sat around and ate, talked, laughed, and then ate, talked, and laughed some more. Each of them appeared happy to get away from their typical days and enjoyed spending time with one another.

Out of all the housewives, Peyton and Derek had the most money. Granted, all of them were rich beyond measure, but with Peyton already being loaded and when Derek sold his first app he reportedly made millions. Now from what Peyton just shared with the ladies, he was about to release another successful App that techies were already vying to buy. Peyton said this one could rake in close to a half billion dollars for Derek! Their money made the rest of them look like paupers.

The housewives sat outside on the private beachfront, sipping on their virgin daiquiris and margaritas. The wind was brisk, causing their hair to blow against their faces.

"When is Harper coming back?" Peyton asked.

"He came back a few days ago, but he just flew right back out of town a couple of hours ago. This time he's traveling with his television show. They're going to small towns all over the country filming and interviewing people who have survived major heart attacks or health scares. He'll be gone for another few weeks."

"He's taking a lot of time off from Adverse General isn't he?"

"Yeah, but he's still able to fulfill his responsibilities as Chief Medical Director. Technology makes that easy. The only thing he can't do is surgery, of course. Plus, Harper is a more than generous donor to that hospital so they're not going to ruffle his feathers…not to mention the connections he has with those who wouldn't stand for him to be booted out of that position."

"I heard that," said Peyton. "I know you're missing him," Peyton said like she was fishing for some answers.

Eva shrugged "You know what, I never thought I'd say this, but I'm used to it."

"Yeah, girl but sleeping alone in that big bed night after night has to be hard. You're a young girl. I know you want to get your groove on."

"No worries. We make up for lost time when he is in town," Eva quickly responded, knowing full well that she was partially lying. Truth be told, Harper usually wanted to have sex like a rabbit when he returned home, but it wasn't like he did it because he missed her. It was more like he wanted to see if she had been with someone else. She didn't know why she felt that way about their sex life, but she did. Yet, she gave him whatever he wanted to keep him at peace.

"I heard that. Sounds like something's up with that," Peyton pushed.

"She told you what was up," Avery spoke up. "So why don't

you just shut up and back off, Peyton. You talk too daggone much."

"Okay, ladies. Let's not do this. We haven't enjoyed each other's company in a while. No need to ruin it with bickering," Meesha intervened.

"If we didn't do that then it wouldn't be us," Avery retorted.

"Well, since you don't want me to say anything to your bestie over there, tell us how are you doing, Miss Thang?" Peyton reverted her attention to Avery. "You're glowing."

Avery smiled. "Ryker and I are great. I'm not dealing with PPD anymore. The kids are happy, the hubby is happy, and that makes me happy."

"Good for you," Meesha said.

Avery snapped her neck around and looked at Meesha like she was surprised to hear her wish her well.

"Thanks, Meesha, which brings us to you. How are you and Carlton? From what I see on Sundays seems like you two are doing good, too," Avery said and smiled.

"Yeah, how *are* you and Carlton?" Eva asked, looking at Meesha with suspicion. "Girl, you got that man preaching like a new kid on the block."

"I keep waiting on him to break out in one of those New Edition dances," added Peyton.

All the ladies broke out into loud laughter.

"You can't talk, lady," said Meesha. "I keep expecting Derek to jump off the bench and do one of those two step hallelujah moves."

Avery laughed louder than any of them.

"Hold up, Avery. We haven't forgotten about Attorney Mitchelson," Peyton mocked.

"Yep, you must be putting that whip appeal on him 'cause it sounded like you had that man speaking in tongues last Sunday."

The ladies laughed hard and long. It felt good to be surrounded by one another.

Eva looked over at Avery. She felt happy for her best friend. She was thrilled when Avery told her that RJ wasn't Carlton's kid, but she still thought that Carlton got off scot-free. He had hurt Avery deeply, cheated on sweet Meesha, and so far, he'd gotten out of it all without so much as a scratch. Sunday after Sunday he stood in the pulpit preaching the gospel when Eva considered him to be nothing more than a hypocrite.

Lately, Avery kept her distance as much as possible from Carlton. There was a time she would stand in line after church services to shake his hand, but that was no more. Ryker asked her about the change a time or two, but she used the excuse that she needed to go straight to the church nursery to pick up RJ. He must have bought it because he stopped asking her about it, and began to accompany her to go get the little boy and the girls.

No one knew, but Avery was actually terrified of Carlton ever since she made a surprise visit to the church one day, a few weeks ago. She brought RJ with her to the church with the intention of putting Carlton on edge about the truth of the boy's paternity. Things backfired rather quickly.

Carlton ushered her quickly into his office when his administrative assistant told him that she was at the church and said it was urgent that she see him. He was livid. The nerve of her. Behind closed doors, Avery mocked and teased him and then did the unthinkable—she threatened to tell Meesha about their fling.

"I've made up my mind to tell Ryker the truth. If you don't tell Meesha, then I'm going to tell her, too," Avery told him that day.

"You have some nerve, coming up in here and making idle threats. Do you know who I am and what I can do to you?" he said, walking up on her and getting all the way up in her face.

RJ looked at Carlton as the man breathed down on his mother.

"This could be your son and you want to get all up on me? I think not. You should want to know if he's yours or not. Look at him…he looks just like you."

"Lies you tell," Carlton bit back. "That brat looks nothing like me. He could be anybody's kid knowing the way you've made yourself available for every Tom, Dick and Harry."

Avery pushed him with one hand while holding on to RJ with the other, then hauled off and slapped Carlton as hard as she could.

Carlton pushed her against the wall of the office, wrapped his massive hand around her neck, and almost pulled her up off the ground. He held her like that until he saw her struggling to breath, turn a deep purplish red, and she almost dropped her baby. He gave her one last hard push before releasing her.

"Don't you ever come near me again and don't you ever try to pin this brat on me. Do you hear me?" he said, so close to her that spittle flew in her face.

Avery's eyes almost popped out of her head. She was terrified. She had witnessed Carlton's fury firsthand before, but never to this extent. It was only through words that he displayed his anger. He had never laid hands on her like this.

"You know what?" he said, stepping back. "You say this kid is mine, then give him here. Give me my son!" he snatched the baby out of her arms. "I'll take him and I'll raise him as mine."

RJ began crying loudly. "I'll raise him right alongside my other kids. I'll expose you for the lying, crazy, maniacal piece of trash that you are. When I'm done with you, not only will you lose this kid, you won't have those two precious little girls of yours or your poor, unsuspecting husband."

Avery ran up on him, reaching out to grab hold of the crying baby, but Carlton laughed while holding her back with his free hand.

"Give me my baby, Carlton. Please, I'll go. Just give me my son," Avery cried and begged.

"Oh, so now you want to cry. I thought you said this was my kid. I don't know if I want to give him back, Avery."

"Please, I came here to tell you that he isn't your son. He… Ryker is his father."

"Is that so?"

"Yes, I promise. Wait, let me show you. Just don't hurt my baby, Carlton. Pleease…" She frantically pulled off the shoulder bag she carried and then proceeded to rummage through it until she pulled out the piece of paper that showed the DNA results. "Here…see. Look," she sobbed.

Carlton, still holding the squealing baby, snatched the paper out of Avery's hand and began to read the results. A wicked, but satisfying smile appeared on his face as he chuckled out loud. "I knew this brat wasn't mine."

He shoved the kid back into Avery's arms. "Do us all a favor. Finish the job you failed to do last year. Kill yourself," he barked. Next, with gritted teeth, and a balled fist, he opened the office door, looked up and down the hall to make sure no one was there, before pushing her out into the hall, screaming baby and all, slamming the door behind her.

The more Avery pondered over her situation, the more she was grateful that RJ was not Carlton's child. She could have lost out on a good man in Ryker, and seeing the evil side of Carlton, she was so very thankful that she hadn't divulged anything to her husband or to Meesha.

Now that she was legally married after all these years, things between them were better. Avery felt that her marriage was stronger. Maybe it was because for the first time in years, she was happier and she felt fulfilled for once in her life.

Not being married to Ryker all of those years had caused her to have feelings of extreme self-doubt and low self-esteem. Maybe that was the reason she had so easily succumbed to Carlton. She felt that she was not good enough for Ryker or any man. She had given her husband two beautiful girls but he never thought she deserved to officially wear his name. All of that had changed and with her regular monthly visits to her therapist, Avery was learning some great coping skills.

"Peyton, what did you say is going on with you and Derek?" asked Avery.

"Ladies, I'm telling you, I can't complain one bit. You know, after the party, he moved back into the bedroom and let's just say, he's not slacking between the sheets." Peyton laughed again and the other ladies joined in, taking sips of their drinks.

"What about you and Liam? How are you two getting along? I know the teenage years can be rough," Meesha said.

"Actually, we're good, too. That boy has such a gentle spirit. He's really a great kid. He doesn't give us a moment's trouble. I think he has a little girlfriend too," Peyton added.

"Oh, girl, you better watch out. I hope Derek has had the talk with him," said Meesha

"Yes, Derek has had the talk, and I think Liam is a responsible young man."

"It's not Liam I would be worried about," Avery said, interjecting into the conversation. "It's these hot tail girls."

"Yeah, you got that right," Peyton said. "Since we're talking about children, I want you all to tell me what you think about this."

"Think about what?" Meesha asked.

"Yeah, what?" asked Eva.

"I have an appointment with a fertility specialist."

"What? A fertility specialist?" Avery yelped. "For what?"

"Duh, what do you go to a fertility specialist for, Avery?"

"Are you serious?" Avery said. "Surely you can't be thinking about having a baby."

"And why can't she?" Meesha asked.

"I want to give Derek a baby and Liam a brother or sister."

"Why would you want to do that? Liam is sixteen, and you want to have a baby now? Wow, I'm shocked," Avery said. "You're pushing forty!"

"Excuse YOU. You're thirty-nine and you just had RJ, *aaand* for your information, I am thirty-seven years old, that's a long way from forty. I still have eggs! Thank you, ma'am." Peyton said with attitude.

"I say go for it. I wish I could have a baby," said Eva.

"Eva, it's different with you. You're still young enough to have kids. You just have to get that loopy husband of yours to reverse his vasectomy," said Peyton.

"Or dump him and get you one that's good and fertile," Avery mocked.

"Seriously, have you ever been pregnant?" Meesha asked Peyton, refocusing the conversation back on her. "And I'm not trying to be mean. I'm just curious."

"No, I haven't, and I've never been on birth control, except for a very short period of time when I was in high school. I just haven't gotten pregnant."

"Is it Derek? Maybe he's sterile," said Eva.

"No, it's not him. Years ago we both went to fertility specialists and everything was fine for both of us. The doctor had no reason to give for me not getting pregnant. Of course I'm not sure if anything has changed since then. But I should still have eggs left, and I want to try."

"What does Derek say about it?" Avery asked.

"I haven't talked it over with him yet. I want to see what the fertility specialist says first before I approach him with the idea. I wanted to see what you ladies thought about it. I think he'll be all for it."

Meesha shrugged. "I'm like Eva, I say go for it, then. I hope everything works out for you."

"Yeah, do it," said Avery.

"Eva, you're mighty quiet over there. What are you thinking about or should I ask *who* are you thinking about?" Peyton probed. "Quentin Winters?"

Eva reared back in her lounge chair. "Quentin Winters? Where did that come from?"

"Girl, it may have been a while since Derek's party, but I saw you two on the dance floor, all booed up. And since Harper isn't handling his husbandly duties, it's easy to see how a young, beautiful girl like you would set her sights on someone, especially someone like Quentin Winters. The man is a good catch for some lucky girl."

"You keep forgetting. I already have a husband. I've messed up once by cheating on Harper. I wouldn't dare do that again. I met the man one time and now you're trying to pair me up with him. Girl, get a life," Eva snapped, not revealing her relationship with Quentin and the rescue shelter.

Eva had only confided in Avery about her position at the rescue shelter and her blossoming friendship between her and Quentin. Almost every day when she was done with her culinary classes, she darted across the street to Quentin's store. She found the work rewarding. There were times when she saw abused dogs and cats being brought into the shelter and her heart went out to the poor creatures. When she saw them blossom after receiving love and care, she felt proud of the work Quentin and his team were doing. She was glad to be part of it.

Regardless of how he made butterflies flitter in her belly every time she was around him, she had learned not to cross Harper. She would never take that chance again.

"Yeah, that's it. Maybe it's time you reevaluated your marriage. You haven't seemed happy ever since you went back to him," said Peyton.

"I'm not one to advocate separating or divorcing so I can't tell you what to do. If he's abusive, then that's a different story or if he's committing adultery, then you have a way out," Meesha explained.

Avery eyed Eva knowingly and Eva eyed her back. The other ladies had no earthly idea about Harper, and days like today made her glad they didn't know. She wouldn't be able to withstand their criticism, judgment, or their pity.

"I just want to finish culinary school," Eva said sadly.

Avery got up from her chair and walked over to the large table filled with food. She made herself a nice sized plate and began chomping on the food as soon as she placed it on her dish. "Ummmm, this is delicious. Eva, I bet yours is going to taste even better. Say, when are you going to make lunch or dinner for us?"

"I don't know. You all have to let me know and I'll be glad to conjure up one of my delectable dishes," Eva said, smiling and sounding more cheerful than she had since she arrived.

"I'm in," said Avery.

"Agreed," said Peyton, raising a glass of ice water to the sky.

"Cool," said Meesha.

"All right, ladies…it's settled. Next ladies' day out will be at my house. I'm going to whip up something that will make you never want to eat anything but Eva's cooking ever again!"

The ladies laughed, clinked their glasses together, raised them in the air, and toasted, "To the Real Housewives of Adverse City."

Words from the Author

If for any reason you believe that having money is the solution to all of your problems, then the characters of "The Real Housewives of Adverse City" should show you otherwise. There are some things money can hide, can make disappear, or bring temporary happiness. Yet, there are some things that we live with each day and even if we have money, and plenty of it, it will never bring us true peace of mind and satisfaction.

We all have problems and situations in life that can cause us grief, anger, and pain. Sometimes those of us who are in financial straits believe that money will bring an end to all of our worldly problems. Again, sometimes money *can* solve problems, but what about those things we wrestle with on the inside? What about the problems and secrets that no one knows about but you? There are some things I still deal with in my life that nobody knows about but me. All the money in the world can't erase them or make them go away. Nothing can remove them from my mind or thoughts unless God does it.

The good news is that nothing that we have done is too tainted, too horrible, or too bad that we cannot be forgiven, and it has nothing to do with the size of our bank accounts. No matter whether you have lot of money or if you don't have a dime, remember the true answer to happiness and peace of mind is found within. Seek God first in all you do. Ask Him to direct your paths. Ask Him for forgiveness for the mistakes you have made and move forward with your life.

This is My Confession
My name is Shelia Bell. I confess that
I am a writer. I am an author.
I am God's amazing girl.
I confess that I write perfect stores
about imperfect people like
The McCoys, The Grahams, The Housewives
and guess what?
Like Me….and YOU!

Thank you for reading another Shelia E. Bell novel

More Titles by Shelia Bell
Some titles are written under Shelia Lipsey

<u>Young Adult Titles</u>
House of Cars
The Life of Payne
The Lollipop Girls
Fifteen (Coming Winter 2018)
The Righteous Brothers (Coming Winter 2018)

<u>Novels</u>
Show A Little Love (*out of print*)
Always Now and Forever Love Hurts
Into Each Life
Sinsatiable
What's Blood Got To Do With It?
Only In My Dreams
Cross Road (Coming Summer 2018)
Forever Ain't Enough (Coming Summer 2018)

<u>Series Books</u>

Beautiful Ugly
True Beauty (*sequel to Beautiful Ugly*)

<u>My Son's Wife Series</u>
My Son's Wife
My Son's Ex-Wife: The Aftermath
My Son's Next Wife
My Sister My Momma My Wife
My Wife My Baby…And Him
The McCoys of Holy Rock
Dem McCoy Boys
My Brother, Father…And Me

<u>*Adverse City Series*</u>
The Real Housewives of Adverse City
The Real Housewives of Adverse City 2
The Real Housewives of Adverse City 3
The Real Housewives of Adverse City 4 (Fall 2018)

<u>*Anthologies*</u>
Bended Knees
Weary to Will
Learning to Love Me

<u>*Nonfiction*</u>
A Christian's Perspective: Journey Through Grief
How to Live Your Life Like It's Golden

Contact information
www.sheliaebell.net
www.sheliawritesbooks.com
sheliawritesbooks@yahoo.com
www.facebook.com/sheliawritesbooks
@sheliaebell (Twitter & Instagram)
@literacyrocks (Instagram)

Please join my mailing list for literary updates and new book release information
www.sheliawritesbooks.com

IF YOU ENJOYED THIS BOOK PLEASE GO TO YOUR FAVORITE REVIEW SITE AND LEAVE A POSITIVE REVIEW